Spider
in the
Sink

Also by Celestine Sibley

Spider in the Sink

A Kate Mulcay Mystery

CELESTINE SIBLEY

EOF
C.11

HarperCollins*Publishers*

HarperCollins books may be purchased for educational, business, or sales promotional use. For information please write: Special Markets Department, HarperCollins Publishers, Inc., 10 East 53rd Street, New York, NY 10022.

FIRST EDITION

Designed by Elina D. Nudelman

Library of Congress Cataloging-in-Publication Data

Sibley, Celestine.
    Spider in the sink / by Celestine Sibley. — 1st ed.
        p. cm.
    ISBN 0-06-017515-X
    I. Title.
    PS3569.I256S6   1997
    813'.54—dc21   97-24071

97 98 99 00 01 ❖/RRD 10 9 8 7 6 5 4 3 2 1

Acknowledgments

With heartfelt gratitude to:

My friend and former editor, Hal Gulliver, for reminding me of the time-worn newspaper rule: When in doubt, take your questions to the top.

The top for several of my problems turned out to be U.S. District Judge Owen Forrester of federal court, who obligingly suspended lofty proceedings long enough to direct one of his bright young law clerks, Lisa Branch, now a practicing attorney, to help me with the law, past and present, on alcohol, tobacco, and firearms.

Commissioner J. Wayne Garner, of the Georgia Department of Corrections, who made me very welcome in my need to get acquainted with the inside of our newest jail. (I knew the old ones.) He not only opened the doors to the prison system to me, but he sent along a superb guide, Officer John Nash, who for thirty years was a foot soldier in the Atlanta Police Department, now retired, and the author of many good stories about how it used to be to be a street cop in our town.

Major Riley Taylor, administrator of the Rice Street prison, who received me hospitably and granted me complete freedom to see and question anything that interested me.

To all of these my profound thanks.

Spider
in the
Sink

Kate Mulcay dragged the plastic garbage full of wild ferns up the hill and collapsed at the top, under a hearts-a-busting-with-love bush. She'd had her eye on hearts-a-busting since fall, when the little bush was loaded with tiny magenta caps, which broke open, spilling out red berries. She'd meant to dig it up and move it to her yard, but its roots seemed to travel under a big rock, and she hadn't been able to move the rock yet.

She propped her feet against the rock and admired it. It was the gray granite that abounds in the woods of north Georgia, but bits of mica, shiny and mirrorlike, flecked its rough flank with silver. She had a place in her yard where she needed that rock—in the bed by the wellhouse, near where she had a watering trough for local dogs and cats and a shade-loving collection of hostas, ferns, and foam flowers. That rock, she mused, would be what the catalogs called an "elegant garden conceit."

She pushed at it with her feet. It didn't budge. She tried moving it with her hands. Its rough surface scratched her palm, causing blood to run.

"Oh, damn!" cried Kate, sucking the blood from her hand. "I need a *man*." She hadn't realized she had said it aloud—not only aloud but loud and clear—until she heard a rustle in the bushes behind her and a masculine voice called out: "Will I do?"

Kate whirled around on the soggy ground, half hoping to see one of her neighbors, somebody who helped out when things at her log cabin threatened to fall apart. It was no neighbor pushing back bushes and coming toward her but a tall, dark-haired man in tennis clothes—white sweater, white shorts, and white shoes—in December, yet, though admittedly it was a warm and sunny December day.

"Oh, hi," said Kate, scrambling to her feet and brushing at the muddy seat of her jeans. "Let's move to the yard." She handed the man her shovel and picked up the plastic garbage bag of ferns.

"Is this what you needed a man for?" the man asked.

Kate gulped in embarrassment. "No, that rock. I want it in my yard."

"Well, let me see." He pushed the blade of the shovel into the earth next to the rock and lifted. It came out easily, and he dropped the shovel and took the rock in his hands. "Where do you want it?"

"Oh, up in the yard," said Kate. "But don't you try

to carry it now. You'll get all dirty. It'll ruin your sweater."

"No matter," said the man, wedging the shovel under his arm and marching up the slope ahead of Kate, the dirty rock clasped to his chest. He eased it down on the ground beside the wellhouse and turned to Kate, brushing leaves and loose dirt off his sweater.

"My, I don't know what to say," said Kate helplessly. "I do want that rock, but your sweater . . . and who did you say you are?"

"Preacher." He grinned at her. "The new Saint Margaret's Episcopal Church. You know—down by the river. We're building, and I came to ask your help."

"And you're the rector?"

"Right," he said, holding out his hand. "Jonathon Craven, reverend."

Kate started to offer her hand, but she looked at the dirt mixed with blood and withdrew it. At the same time, he saw the dirt on his own hand and pulled it back.

"Come on in the house," she said. "Soap and hot water. And can I give you a cup of coffee? Or tea? You're Anglican, I suppose."

"Nothing of the sort," he said quickly. "South Georgia Episcopal. I'll take whatever's available. Coffee's fine."

Kate steered her guest to the kitchen sink and went in search of hand soap and a towel for him. She couldn't help admiring his long-fingered, sun-browned hands as he lathered up. All that tennis, she thought. Men's hands frequently appealed to her, but these were downright beautiful. He moved to give her room at the sink and shared the soap and towel with her. A drop or two of blood started up and ran off her hand, and he took her hand in his and looked at the palm.

"Better put something on this," he said.

"Aw, it's nothing," said Kate. "I scraped it on the rock. It's all right. Let's sit down and have our coffee."

He pulled out a chair for her at the little pine kitchen table and brought cups and the coffeepot from the counter. It was a small gesture, but Kate enjoyed it as something she hadn't had in the years since Benjy, her husband, died. She smiled on Jonathon Craven blissfully. He was handsome, incredibly handsome—very tall, with gray eyes under dark eyebrows and dark hair that, like the rock they'd brought up from the woods, was stippled with silver.

His legs were so long he couldn't get them under the table but pulled his chair back and tilted it, making him look at home. Kate found she was glad for that.

"So Saint Margaret's is already under construction?" she asked.

"Almost finished," he said. "But not paid for. That's why I came to see you."

Oh, oh, Kate thought. He's going to ask for money, and I'm behind with my pledge at the Presbyterian church.

He read her mind. "I'm not asking for money," he

said. "I wondered if you would let us have a tea in your garden and sort of tour."

"My garden?" Kate laughed. "Have you seen it, my garden? It's far from a garden! It's a poor, neglected little weed patch. I'd be ashamed to call it anything so pretentious as a garden, and as for inviting people to come and see it—for pay—I wouldn't dare!"

Across the table, Jonathon Craven quirked a glossy eyebrow at her and grinned. "I hear your roses in June are spectacular," he murmured. "And your herbs a delight. We're going to show some of Roswell's traditional old gardens, but the feeling is that your garden with its log cabin background and its simplicity would be an inspiration to neophytes. And you know"—he ducked his head shyly, as if he were about to say something heretical—"Roswell is simply teeming with newcomers, all eager gardeners."

"Which of the old gardens are you showing?" Kate asked, suddenly interested.

"Miss Maria Beckman's boxwood garden and a place I haven't seen called Hollyhock Hill," he said. "They're both antebellum, I think. At least the houses that go with them are. You know them?"

Kate nodded. She felt better about her own unmanicured patch. Miss Maria's boxwood garden was boxwood, nothing else. Wonderful fragrant old boxwood, but that was all. Would anybody pay to walk through corridors of boxwood? Only loyal friends and money-hungry Episcopalians, she decided. As for Hollyhock Hill, it was, as she remembered, an organic vegetable garden, encircled by annuals, many of which—but not all—were holly-hocks. If these were to be showpieces, she thought, her own herbs and roses, with luck, wouldn't look too bad. Simple, but simplicity was what the preacher wanted, he claimed.

"Let me think about it," she said at last. "You may know I work for the newspaper every day, and I have no help in the yard. Except"—she grinned—"when a preacher hears my plea and hauls up a big rock for me."

"This preacher will be glad to help you anytime," he said seriously. "I have no family, and there are hours in most days when I could lend a hand in your garden. Just call on me. I can cut grass and dig holes and prune. I was raised by a gardening mother in south Georgia."

Kate didn't think she would be calling on him. She wouldn't want those smooth brown long-fingered hands manning the shovel again. But maybe he *was* a gardener. "Where in south Georgia do you come from?"

"Valdosta."

"Day lilies," Kate said. "The hemerocallis capital of the world."

"Right!" He offered a congratulatory smile. "You know Valdosta? My mother had dozens of different varieties of day lilies. Do you grow them too?"

"A few," Kate said cautiously. It wasn't the time or place, she told herself, to admit that she had tried and failed with day lilies and didn't plant them any-more. They bloomed for such a short period, she had found, and then put up spiky dry stalks out of great useless hummocks of space-grabbing green foliage.

"And you have no family here, you say?" she asked.

"Divorced," he replied. "That's why I'm here. To build a new church and assemble a congregation presumably liberal enough to put up with a divorced rector."

"Ah," said Kate, with real sympathy. "Is it working out?"

"So far." He shrugged his big shoulders. "I think they forgive much because I've been diligent with hammer and nails. We've built the church ourselves, and I have hammered gray shingles harder than Sunday homilies. But now—"

"Now you have to settle down and preach," Kate finished.

"Exactly."

"Well, I'd like to see the church—and of course I want to hear you hammer those homilies," Kate said, smiling.

"Naturally. We expect you, especially since we've asked you to help us. And you will consider it, won't you?"

"Oh, I will. And I'm honored to be asked. You can see it's nothing of a garden, but if I can get it spruced up a bit by June . . . it is June when you want to do the tea and tour, isn't it?"

"Second week. A time, they tell me, of flawless weather."

"Most of the old roses are at their best then," Kate admitted. "Well, I'll think about it and let you know."

"I do thank you." He put down his coffee cup and stood up. "Saint Margaret's will thank you too."

Kate walked with him to the backyard, where she was surprised to see a truck parked. Not one of the nifty, slick paint-and-chrome compact vehicles that had become fully as stylish with young couples as BMWs and Jaguars, but an old and weary Ford, with patches of missing paint and a couple of sagging fenders.

He saw her glance, and he laughed. "You're wondering if it's mine?" he said. "It is. Every dent, every scrap of rust."

"Just not an Episcopal-looking vehicle," Kate offered, grinning.

"You mean it's not elegant and sort of sedate? Well, it isn't the church's. I arrived with it, and it has proved itself a very useful old truck. We've hauled tons of shingles in it and . . . well, it's all I have. My wife got the car in the divorce."

"I'm sorry," murmured Kate, unable to think of anything else to say, but she did admire his loyalty to the old vehicle. "I like a truck," she added. "And you really need one if you live in the country. Where *do* you live?"

"Almost country. It's the guesthouse back of Dr. Miller's river house. Really not much more than a little shack in the woods. But comfortable enough. And rent free."

He settled his long body on the high truck seat and leaned out over a dusty window to shake Kate's hand.

"It's been a pleasure being with you . . . May I call

you Kate? And I'm Jon. I thank you for the coffee
and the consideration of our garden project. Shall I
expect to see you Sunday?"

Kate nodded. "I'll try to make it." To herself she
said, You're darn tooting I'll make it Sunday. I've
never seen such a good-looking preacher. I'm going
to check this one out.

Kate watched the battered truck out of the driveway and turned to look at her yard, trying to see it as
it would look to Jonathon and paying guests. It
wouldn't do. Here in December, it looked brown and
desiccated. A fine month for wandering in the
woods, gathering pine and cedar for the mantel and
the front door, but still an austere one, without a
pansy or a tulip showing. Kate had meant to get pansies out in the fall, as everybody in Atlanta seemed to
do these days. Apartment complexes and filling sta-
tions and shopping malls had vast voluptuous beds
of pansies, some of them unfortunately planted in
stripes of purple and gold. Kate had put off pansies,
and now she regretted it. They were endearing little
plants and would have made a splash in her bare and
flowerless garden. She was wrong to hold it against
them that they were overdone by commercial
planters. She wished for pansies and tulips now.

As for herbs, why had she always stuck hers in just
anywhere instead of having a picture-book concen-
tration of herbs, such as she had seen in magazines?
She once toyed with the idea of using a big wagon
wheel, with different plants between each set of
spokes. She had even got a wheel somewhere, but it
didn't seem big enough for the number of plants she

had. She thought of rectangles and circles, neatly fenced. But none of these appealed to her. She stuck herbs here and there in flower beds and in pots, where she had room and thought they might be at home. An old cow-feed manger salvaged from a deserted barn down the road held pots of scented geraniums, still looking a bit anemic from having spent a month indoors. A blue cook pot, found at an old house site, held her biggest and most ebullient rosemary. She reached out a finger to touch a branch. Sometimes rosemary went dry, but this was green and left its fragrance on her fingers. Parsley and chives made a green showing by the kitchen steps, and she was almost grateful to the silver wormwood for its sprawl over the stunted, slow-to-bloom fairy rose.

The old brick terrace beside the wellhouse pleased her. She supposed it was where they would put small tables and serve tea. Benjy, her husband, had salvaged the bricks from an old building downtown, where they had been through the occupation by General Sherman's men and had survived, barely, the burning of Atlanta. Some of them were soft and crumbly, some of them were cracked. Grass and weeds came up between them, but Kate loved to spend a sunny morning sprawling on the bricks and hand weeding, giving room, she always hoped, to a tiny flat variety of thyme, which took over in spots. She bent down now to look for the thyme. It would count as an herb for the visitors, and to her delight it seemed to be spreading. She had months to get ready for the church's show, and she unexpectedly

Celestine
Sibley

seemed to have decided that she would do it. She would make a plan and draw up plant lists.

Kate spent the week torn between getting her yard in shape and getting herself in shape to see Jon again. She bought a new suit—cream wool with café-au-lait trim—and matching suede pumps. She also got a new haircut, shorter and fluffier than she had had before, and experimented with a new lipstick.

Dropping by the *Roswell Neighbor,* the weekly newspaper, she made an excuse for checking back issues, looking for and finally finding the little story that had run announcing the arrival of the Reverend Jonathon Craven. He was forty-five years old, only a few years her junior, a graduate of Duke University who had studied theology at Sewanee in Tennessee. He had been married to Valerie Kent, the television actress; they had no children. His parents, residents of Valdosta, Georgia, were dead.

Toward the end of the week, Kate began to wish she had got her log cabin all garlanded and greener-ied in anticipation of Christmas and assembled some food to invite the minister and maybe one or two other people for a small Sunday-night party. Getting the cabin Christmasy was easy, something she had continued to do even after the death of Benjy, when presumably she would be alone for the holiday. She never had been. There were always people to invite, what her office friends called "Kate's orphans and outcasts."

It was always the same. She put a fat pine wreath with a big red velvet bow on the front door and dressed the mantel with pine and magnolia boughs, interspersed with carefully polished red apples. Her only tree was a small one in the kitchen, decorated entirely with miniature kitchen utensils given to her years before by an antiques-happy friend, who had had a go at collecting the tiny eggbeaters and thimble-sized egg baskets, before she switched to angels and elves and vintage Santa Clauses and offered the kitchenware to Kate. Kate loved the little tree, especially since she and Benjy on occasional vacation trips found additions to it, an infinitesimal skillet, a perfect wooden rolling pin the size of a baby's finger. She didn't bother with electric lights. They had always used small candles on the tree, and now she used masses of red candles on the tables and on cupboards, to supplement the lively blaze she always managed in the big fireplace.

But she realized when she got to Saint Margaret's on Sunday that her efforts at Christmas decorating were paltry. The little gray church facing the Chattahoochee River had been sumptuously decorated in garlands of green, enormous wreaths and banks of poinsettias filling the sanctuary. There was the usual advent wreath, with three purple candles and the white one to be lighted on Christmas morning—much handsomer than the ones Kate remembered making. Sprays of cedar and pine filled the windowsills, with a candle burning in each, picking out the colors of the stained-glass windows.

The church smelled of new lumber and damp

stone. Its dark timbered rafters were entwined with garlands of pine, white angels the size of butterflies mounted on them. The congregation was small, running to a dozen families and a handful of elderly couples, some of whom Kate recognized as old-time Roswell residents who had once gone to the Presbyterian church. The new church had not acquired an organ yet, or a choir, but the congregational singing was strong and good, accompanied by a guitar, Kate was surprised to see, in the hands of Jonathon Craven.

In his long black robe and purple stole, he looked like some big exotic bird, until he stepped down to the floor and faced the congregation with his guitar. He smiled gently and struck a chord, and the sweet, mellow strains of "O Come All Ye Faithful" filled the little church. When he mounted to the pulpit, resting his guitar in one of the pulpit chairs, he turned and quirked an eyebrow in what Kate could have sworn was her direction. He had seen and recognized her.

He read from the Bible. Kate, checking the little printed church bulletin, found it was from Ephesians, a passage about being "rooted and grounded in love," which would make you able to "comprehend what is the breadth and length and depth and height . . . that ye might be filled with the fullness of God."

His sermon subject was listed as "The Experiment of Christianity," and Kate listened intently, enjoying the deep music of his voice more than following his words, which seemed to concern "this strange and mysterious life" and to advocate the experiment of Christianity "not for a life but for a single blessed hour," reposing trust "which is higher and better than reason."

Kate pushed the words aside, planning to think about them later. Meanwhile, she concentrated on the communion service and the closing hymn. Jonathon lifted his hand in the benediction, which Kate found herself responding to as a blessing real as any she had ever received. The words to the benediction were familiar. She had been hearing them all her life. But when Jonathon Craven lifted his long arm and bowed his head and intoned: "The Lord bless thee and keep thee; the Lord make his face to shine upon thee and be gracious unto thee. The Lord lift up his countenance upon thee and give thee peace: the peace of God, which passeth all understanding. Keep your hearts and minds in the knowledge and love of God, and of his son, Jesus Christ our Lord; and the blessing of God Almighty, the father, the son and the holy ghost, be amongst you and remain with you always"—Kate felt tears gathering in her eyes and a surge of happiness. The benediction was no more than it had ever been, the closing words of a minister, but she felt that as spoken by this man, they carried hope and truth.

A small crowd gathered around the minister on the church steps, and Kate awaited her turn.

"Ah, Kate, it's good to have you here," he said, holding her hand.

"I like your church," Kate said, and then, daringly, "And you're good. I'm glad I came."

"Can you wait a minute?" he asked, as a group of teenage girls approached.

Kate nodded and stepped aside. There were three of them, all young and beautiful. The one with the long blond hair cascading over her shoulders was first in line to shake his hand and was gushing, "Oh, Father Craven, you're cool! I want to try everything you suggested!"

"Me too," echoed the plump redhead beside her. "And you play a mean guitar."

The third girl was smaller and incredibly pretty, Kate thought. She had soft brown curly hair, held back from a heart-shaped face with a ribbon, and meltingly beautiful brown eyes. She said nothing but offered the minister a small gloved hand and looked up into his face with total adoration.

He seemed shaken by this one. "Your names," he said. "Tell me your names."

The blonde spoke up. "I'm Hettie."

The redhead said, "I'm Cece for Cecilia, and she's"—bobbing her head toward the third one—

"I'll tell him myself," the girl said decisively. "I'm Harriet Amelia Marylinn Caroline Amy Todd Dickson."

"Whew!" said the minister, laughing. The girls laughed too.

"She just didn't want you to find out she's called Toddy by everybody," said Hettie.

"I don't blame you, with a beautiful name like Harriet Amelia Marylinn Caroline Amy." He recited the names glibly.

The girl had a dazzling white smile, and she turned the radiance of her brown eyes on him. "Thank you," she said demurely.

Jonathon seemed to have forgotten that he had asked Kate to wait. He took the girl's hand and turned it gently in his own.

"I hope you girls will come often," he said.

Other congregants were collecting, waiting to speak to him, and he smiled winsomely at them without doing anything to move the girls along. When at last they came near to Kate, she heard one of them say, "Isn't he a hunk?"

"He looks like John Kennedy, Jr. . . ."

"Oh, he does!" said Cece, sighing deeply. "I think I want him for Christmas."

"No, me," said Hettie. "I saw him first. My mother was on the pulpit committee, and she brought him to our house for dinner before he even said he'd accept their call."

"You all have nerve," said Toddy, tossing her curls. "He'll be the one to decide, and it'll probably be some old lady in her forties."

"God willing," Kate said to herself, and moved forward to a gap in the line in front of the minister.

"Kate," he said shyly. "I wanted to ask you to have dinner with me tonight. I caught some fish yesterday, and we could cook them on the grill in my backyard."

"Fine," said Kate. "What time, and what can I bring?"

"Only yourself," he said, smiling. "Five-thirty or six all right? We should still have some sun on the river that early."

Kate drove back to her log cabin in a state of high excitement. A date . . . she had a date! She went out to dinner occasionally with men from the office, but this was different: not a coworker, not a longtime colleague who would probably want to confide in her about his love life, but a handsome stranger, an impressive man of the cloth, who had asked her to his house! She wondered if she should take a salad or a bottle of wine. And what should she wear—pants? a skirt and sweater? For once Kate Mulcay felt the need of a girlfriend to call and consult. She lived such an independent life, and to tell the truth, she never had girlish confidences to share with another woman. Until now. She felt like one of the teenagers who had clustered around him. A hunk, they had called him, a term she thought revolting, but come to think of it, he did look a little like the younger John Kennedy.

Once at the cabin, Kate felt some of her excitement abate. She took another look at her yard, and her spirits fell. It looked winter dreary, beyond rehabilitation by June. She changed from her new church outfit to jeans and collected clippers and a garbage bag for a walk down toward the creek.

Perhaps she should gather some Christmas greens for the preacher—or had the ladies of the church already done up his cottage? The church had looked so beautiful it stood to reason that they wouldn't have left the temporary vicarage undecorated. She thought of the hearts-a-busting-with-love bush. Although she had planned to put it in her yard, it would be a pleasant irony to give it to the preacher, who was probably already aware of hearts a-busting in his congregation.

Kate found the bush shallow-rooted in the spot where the rock had been and dug it up with her hands, careful to keep its fine roots covered and its thin green trunk well supported so it would not break in the journey back up the hill. She soaked paper towels to wrap around it and enclosed the whole thing in plastic. She stowed it in the back seat of her car and went in to take a shower.

To her own surprise, Kate, who seldom dressed up beyond a suit or a skirt and sweater, found herself donning a long flowered skirt and her best silk shirt.

Hearts-a-busting-with-love and a long silk skirt for a backyard cookout! She must have lost her mind. She should change to jeans, and she would certainly not tell the preacher the country name for the little bush. It was said the Indians called it wahoo, and that's what she would tell him. In the end, she stuck with the silk skirt and even added her favorite string of pearls, an anniversary gift from Benjy years ago.

The sun was still on the river when Kate drove up in front of Dr. Miller's driveway, looking for access to the guesthouse in the backyard. She stopped and let the motor idle while she looked at the setting sun, which had turned the Chattahoochee into a river of flame. Winter sunsets were an almost daily delight to Kate. She sat late in her own backyard to witness the flamboyant departure of the sun over hill and pine trees. But how much better was the show with the murky waters of the old Chattahoochee in the foreground. She wished she had come earlier. She was wondering if Jonathon Craven had been watching the sunset, when he tapped on the car window and stood smiling at her.

"I'm glad you made the sunset," he said. "Pull in the driveway. It circles around the big house and will bring you out beside my humble abode. Park anywhere. There's plenty of room."

He had called it a shack, but the house he got rent free from Dr. Miller was better than that—a former stable transformed by rough boards and dark-green stain into a sort of rustic ranch house, long and narrow, with a lot of windows looking out on Dr. Miller's camellia garden, the river barely visible at the corner of the big house. Jonathon strode ahead of Kate, motioned her to stop at the front door, and hurried to open the car door for her. He offered her a hand, but Kate turned and reached for the plastic-wrapped hearts-a-busting plant. His big hand was there ahead of hers.

"You brought this to me? What a nice guest! What is it?"

"You might have preferred a covered dish," Kate said, sliding out of the car and straightening her flowered skirt. "But if we can make this grow, you'll love it. It's called heart—" She stopped. She hadn't meant to tell him that name. "Wahoo bush," she amended.

"You started to say 'heart' something," Jon said, his gray eyes fixed on her face.

"Well Hearts-a-busting-with-love," Kate said. "That's what country people call it. It has an unusual bloom—a sort of little fuchsia cap that pops open in the late summer or fall, spilling out a lot of red seeds."

"Wonderful name," Jonathon said. "I hope I can make it grow."

"You're entitled to it," said Kate, smiling. "You lifted the rock off its roots. It likes partial shade. You want me to help you pick a spot?"

"I'd appreciate it," the minister said. "Let's look now, before it gets dark. I can dig the hole in the morning."

They walked together around the corner of the house, where a terrace of river rock had been laid and a charcoal grill sent up a plume of fragrant smoke around the fillets of five trout.

"My, what a lot of fish!" said Kate. "We can't eat that many, can we? Do you have other guests?"

"Nope," said Jonathon. "I just wanted you." His face was solemn, his gray eyes were fixed on hers with a grave expression that Kate found brought a flush to her cheeks and made her duck her head in embarrassment. "If we can't eat the fish," Jonathon went on, "I have a cat. I caught 'em, and I didn't know what else to do with them."

Kate welcomed the introduction of the cat into the conversation.

The plates were set on a counter in the small kitchen, and there was a decanter of wine and two glasses on the coffee table in front of a denim-covered sofa.

"Sherry?" said Jonathon, lifting the decanter inquiringly.

Kate nodded. "Thank you," she said, looking around the room. The wall opposite the front windows was all bookshelves, crammed full. Kate wandered closer to examine the titles. They seemed to run to theology and sermons.

She ran a finger along the titles and the names of authors. "The Reverend Augustus Toplady," she read aloud. "What a name! Who is he?"

"I think a poet," said Jonathon. "Lived about the time of the American Revolution. The only thing I remember is a four-liner I learned in school: 'When we in darkness walk,/Nor feel the heavenly flame,/Then is the time to trust our God/And rest upon His name.'"

"I suppose we all walk in darkness from time to time," Kate ventured, putting Mr. Toplady's book back on the shelf and reaching for another.

"Yes, I suppose," said the preacher, sighing heavily and taking a sip of his sherry.

"Here's Saint Augustine, of course," said Kate, "and Thomas à Kempis, and my friend Phillips Brooks. I've read some of his sermons. And Carlyle and Martin Luther and"—she lifted a slender volume from the shelf and laughed aloud—"and Edna St. Vincent Millay! She's my favorite, but isn't she a funny choice for a minister? All that carnal love!"

Jonathon grinned shyly and refilled her sherry glass. "Except for the fact that it gets us into trouble sometimes, carnal love is as desirable for preachers as it is for poets."

Kate looked carefully out the window and returned Millay's sonnets to the bookshelf.

"Let's eat," she said. Things were moving a little *too* quickly. She thought it time to retreat. She was certain of it when Jonathon picked up a platter and turned to the door, stopping en route to kiss her on the forehead.

"I'm glad you're here," he said softly, "and it's nice to have a girl who knows Millay."

Kate looked at him, aghast. "To have a girl," he'd said. She was not a girl, many years past it, and the possessive verb didn't ring true. He didn't "have" her. Or did he? She felt encircled in the little house, in the light from his lamps and the fragrance of the supper he was cooking. She felt captive to his voice reciting poetry.

Hearing his voice in the backyard, she thought he was talking to his cat. "Caught you!" he said. "What are you doing here?"

She walked to the kitchen door. Standing beside Jonathon at the cooker were the three teenagers who had been in the reception line at the morning church service.

The blonde, Hettie, spoke up. "We were just passing by and we smelled your trout cooking. You have so much—five big ones—we were hoping you might want to share."

"But you aren't invited, now, are you?" Jonathon said in a kind but firm voice.

"We know," said the pretty one called Toddy, looking sorrowful. "But since you have so much and only one other guest . . ." They must have been looking in the window. They had probably seen Jonathon kiss her.

Kate wanted to open the screen door and yell "Git!" at the girls, but it was Jonathon's business. She would let him handle it. He handled it by saying,

"Okay. I suppose it's all right, since Miss Kate is here
to chaperone. Go on inside and ask her to get out the
paper plates. I only have two good plates, and she
and I are using those."

"Oh, you!" cried the redhead, pushing at him
playfully and heading for the kitchen. Kate stepped
back from the door to let them in, and they came,
jostling one another and smiling happily.

Jonathon gestured helplessly to her.

She felt demoted. Now she was a chaperone and
not his girl. She had an impulse to flee, to get in her
car and drive away, leaving him to his adoring claque
of young maidens. The five of them took plates and
settled themselves about the room on the sofa and
the two overstuffed chairs. Jonathon, who had set
the table on the kitchen counter, seemed not to
mind. He talked to the girls, asking questions about
where they went to school—all attended the local
high school—what their parents did, where they
lived, and how they happened to be walking by the
river on a chill December afternoon.

Kate listened patiently. It was her bad luck to be
the age of some of the parents and to know where
they lived. As to why the girls were walking by the
river, Toddy, the little beauty, answered promptly in
her soft voice.

"We wanted to see you," she murmured, lifting
her brown eyes to his face.

The minister had the grace to look embarrassed.
"Well, now," he said easily, "there's no dessert, and
it's getting dark. I think you all should head home."

"First we'll clear away," said Hettie. "You want

these plates in the garbage and these leftovers for your cat?"

Jonathon protested that he would do the clearing, but reared by generations of women who had run church suppers, the three smiled sweetly and ignored his protests. When they had washed the silver and the glasses, Hettie dried her hands and turned to Kate.

"It *is* getting dark," she said. "If you're going our way, would you mind dropping us off?"

Little rascal, Kate said to herself.

"Oh, you mustn't go," Jonathon said. "We've only begun to talk."

Kate looked at the watchful faces of the girls. They want me to go, she thought wryly. They ruined my visit, and now they are determined to get me out of here. Suddenly she didn't care. She felt ready to go.

Oddly enough, she had a feeling Jonathon was ready for her to leave. He followed them to the car, opening the door for Kate on the driver's side while the girls waited by the back door.

"Oh, excuse me," he said, obviously surprised that they waited to be handed in. And then they showed him why. Cece and Hettie each grabbed him around the waist and kissed him on the cheek. Toddy planted one right on his mouth, before jumping, laughing, into Kate's car.

Celestine
Sibley

"Girls!" cried Jonathon, sternly. "You shouldn't have done that!" He wiped his mouth with the back of his hand and glared at the threesome, but his gray eyes reflected amusement rather than annoyance, Kate thought.

She started the car and leaned out the window.

25

"Thank you for the good dinner," she said. Then, for the benefit of the girls, "and everything else."

The minister lifted his hand in a salute and watched them drive off.

Back at her cabin, Kate dropped the flowered skirt on the floor and stepped out of it. A lot of good you did me! she said silently.

The phone was ringing when Kate came inside from putting out a late supper for Pepper and Sugar, her dog and cat.

"Oh, Kate," said Jonathon, sighing heavily. "I'm so sorry our time together turned into the children's hour. I had no idea . . ."

"Perfectly all right," said Kate insincerely. "They're hardly children—from those kisses I saw them give you. But they are charming, and I don't blame you for being captivated by them. All that adoration . . ."

"I am *not* captivated by them!" the preacher said defensively. "You are far more interesting to me. We have been down the road together."

"I think I've covered more road—and years—than you have," Kate said, so tired now she would have told him her age if he had asked. He didn't ask.

"Could I see you tomorrow?" he said instead. "Lunch? Dinner? Anytime you're free?"

"I don't think so," said Kate. "Tomorrow's a work-day for me."

"I could come by your office," Jonathon offered. "I'd love to see where you work."

"Let's make it another time, if you don't mind," said Kate. "I don't have any idea what the day holds for me, and I may be out of the office most of the time."

"How about tomorrow night, then? I will see you at home when you get off," Jonathon said decisively. "About six o'clock all right?"

"Let's say Wednesday," Kate said, uncertainly. Things seemed to be progressing too quickly with Jonathon. She needed time to accommodate herself to a possible relationship.

Kate went off to bed without washing her face. The way things were going, she figured Elizabeth Arden with all her sweet-smelling unguent artillery couldn't make her look good enough to compete with three teenage girls. She had just picked up a new Kathy Trocheck murder mystery, when she changed her mind. After all, he was insisting on seeing her and making noises about the road they had traveled together. She got up and washed her face and anointed it lavishly with something that professed to banish wrinkles and dry skin.

Wednesday was one of those deceptively ordinary newspaper days. She was running late, and all the spaces in the company parking lot were taken. The new security guard would have sent her two blocks away to a truck lot, but David, the commanding officer of the security forces, was mindful of her long tenure, and said, "Gimme your keys, hon, and I'll park it for you as soon as there's room." She climbed the hill to the front door, wondering if that was the tip-off on how the day would go. There wouldn't, however, be a David at every juncture to save her.

Her answering machine held eighteen messages, including the inevitable one from Miss Iris Moon about street people. She and Kate had been jointly concerned about a Vietnam veteran who sat with his dog at the curbside across from the newspaper office every day, his knitted cap held out with a few representational coins in it.

Kate had gone out and interviewed him, and his story ran in her column, with a picture of him and his dog, Foodstamp. No shelter would take Shag in if he refused to give up Foodstamp, and he did refuse. He had been wounded in Vietnam and had a Purple Heart to show for it. Why, Kate asked, wouldn't the Veterans Administration take care of him? The question was repeated by numbers of readers, including Miss Iris Moon, but the VA had its reasons. Shag spent the money passersby put in his cap on cheap wine and was frequently so drunk only the hospital, where he could be securely tied to a bed, would have him. And what about Foodstamp?

Sympathizers in the newsroom and a young man who worked in the bank down the street took turns inviting Foodstamp home with them, but Shag took his dog back whenever he returned to the street, and Miss Iris Moon called Kate daily to inquire about the animal's well-being. She knitted a coat for him, which the big golden retriever refused to wear. She sent dog biscuits and occasionally a five-dollar bill for his master. Mindful of Shag's tendency to spend it on wine, Kate changed the five dollars into ones and rationed them out. It hadn't worked. People in the neighborhood were surprisingly generous. Once, Kate was standing on the corner talking to Shag when a woman dropped ten dollars in his cap.

Shag and Foodstamp had recently picked up a companion—a little bearded man with bright-blue eyes and a wart on his nose—whom Shag had tactlessly but accurately nicknamed "Warty." According to Robin McDonald, one of the police reporters, who had experience in such matters, he was a veteran not of Vietnam but of the jailhouse. A petty criminal, he had telltale tattoos on his arms, she said.

They seemed a congenial pair, and Kate felt that they might keep each other warm at night in the lumber pile across the street from Saint Luke's Episcopal Church, where Shag had established his headquarters.

Kate was halfway through retrieving her messages when the phone rang. It was Miss Iris Moon.

"Kate," said Miss Moon imperiously, "you know that Christmas is coming. I'm sitting up here in this big house by myself, and I've decided to give Shag and Warty my guesthouse."

"I don't think you should," Kate began uncertainly. The two street fellows were pretty dirty and would almost certainly be drunk. Kate felt a measure of responsibility, since it was her column that had called Miss Moon's attention to the pair.

"Don't be a detractor," Miss Moon commanded. "It's almost Christmas, and there they are out on the

street just because they love a dog. As a dog lover myself—I'm on the board of the Humane Society, you know—I feel compelled to do something."

"Bless your heart," said Kate, suddenly touched by the older woman's kindness. "Although I can't say I agree with this. Shall I tell them?"

"No," said Miss Moon decisively. "I'm coming to get them myself. I'll have my man stop my car in front of your building, and if you'll meet me there, we can walk across the street together. I'm leaving now!"

"Oh Lordy," moaned Kate. She didn't know where Miss Moon lived or how long it would take her to get to town. And Kate did have work to do. She called her friend David the security officer.

"She's an older woman in a big car—I think chauffeur-driven. Will you let her park for a few minutes? She's coming to get Shag and Warty."

"Thank the Lord," said David. "Anything to remove them from our landscape! The police won't have them, and they're sitting out there polluting this end of town."

"Thank you, David," said Kate softly. "I'll be right down."

The limousine that pulled up in front of the *Atlanta Searchlight* an hour later seemed half a block long and was driven by a handsome uniformed chauffeur. He leapt to the street and hurried around to open a rear door for an elegant white-haired woman in mink.

"Kate Mulcay?" she said. "I'm Iris Moon. Give me your arm, honey. I *would* wear these silly shoes today." The silly shoes looked to Kate to be about a size two, with perilously high heels.

"You're dressed for the holiday," Kate said, holding out her arm.

"One does hope to look a little dressed up at this season," Miss Moon said, her eyes falling on Kate's battered loafers.

"My country shoes," Kate said hastily. "I have my town shoes under my desk."

She moved slowly to the corner, with Miss Moon clinging to her arm. Shag and Warty, leaning against the building across the street, waved cordially. The traffic light changed to green, and Kate attempted to move a little faster. She wished one of them—the chauffeur or David or even Shag or Warty—would help her get Miss Moon across the street. Her arm, latched onto Kate's, grew increasingly heavy, and she rocked on the silly shoes as if the next step would plunge her to the concrete street.

Shag was standing, and he looked surprisingly neat and clean, as if he'd been expecting a benefactor. His beard had been trimmed. Even the boots he wore, usually muddy, had been brushed. Warty, on the other hand, lay crumpled against the building like a dirty rag doll, his blue eyes wandering from side to side. Foodstamp, the great golden retriever, leaned against Shag's legs and wagged a welcoming tail at Kate and her companion.

Kate made introductions. "Shag, Warty, this is Miss Iris Moon. She has come to invite you to spend Christmas with her."

Shag didn't hesitate. He bowed from the waist and

Celestine
Sibley

reached for Miss Moon's hand. "Ma'am," he said, "this is an unexpected pleasure." He lifted the hand to his lips, and the woman made no effort to retrieve it. Warty scrambled to his feet and stood at full attention. "Ma'am," he said, offering a mock salute.

"Well, aren't you young men absolutely charming!" Miss Moon said. "Let's get in the car." She lifted a hand, and by some miracle, the handsome chauffeur picked the signal out of the confusion of traffic and brought the big car across the street, to halt beside them. He looked at Shag and Warty distastefully as he opened a door and helped Miss Moon, on her rickety shoes, into the passenger compartment. With studied indifference, he turned his back while Shag and Warty scrambled in, shifting the two white plastic paint buckets that contained all their possessions on the velvet seats, while the big dog sat panting on the plush carpet. The chauffeur climbed in and revved up the engine, and suddenly they were off, Foodstamp raising his paws to the back of the driver's velvet-covered seat and barking ecstatically. Shag, apparently feeling that the occasion called for something ceremonious, took off his knitted cap and bowed deeply to Kate as the limo pulled away from the curb.

Late in the day, after Kate had answered a few letters and cleared her computer screen of her latest column, she had a phone call from Philip Brown, a lawyer she used to have coffee with in the days when she covered the courthouse. She didn't have much legal business, so their encounters were infrequent. A pleasant young man, the son and grandson of judges, he was appointed occasionally to represent some indigent defendant. Kate had happened to be present when he was asked to serve as guardian for Miss Millicent Claiborne Clay, who had just been held mentally incompetent and sent to Milledgeville State Hospital.

"I don't think there's a lot of work involved," Phil had remarked to Kate over coffee in the courthouse snack shop. "You remember she had ten thousand dollars tied to her teddies when the police picked her up for being a public nuisance."

Kate had nodded. She did indeed remember most of Miss Millicent's capers, and she did not regard her as a public nuisance. "I know a lot of people who are bigger nuisances than she is," she had told Judge Osborn in one of their coffee sessions after court.

"Right," said the judge amiably. "You knew my first wife?"

Now Phil Brown was calling Kate.

"Do you play the piano?" he asked. Kate snapped back to the present.

"Oh, no," said Kate. "My mother insisted I have lessons, but they didn't take. Why?"

"Because," said the lawyer, chuckling, "you now own twenty-five pianos!"

"Great! What am I supposed to do with twenty-five pianos?"

"You better decide," said Mr. Brown. "You just inherited them."

"That's insane."

"That's Miss Millicent," said her lawyer. "It was her dying wish."

"Miss Millicent can't be dead!"

But the old lady *was* dead, and buried in the hospital's cemetery. And her money was gone. Brown had attended the funeral and would have notified Kate, but he decided the hundred-mile trip so close to Christmas would be an imposition on her.

"The city is getting her house for taxes," he said. "And that leaves the contents for you. You remember how fond of you she became. Want to ride down there and take a look?"

Kate looked at the newsroom clock. Five o'clock, peak traffic time. She might as well go look at the pianos on Bass Street.

Phil Brown, driving an ancient Chevrolet he couldn't bear to part with, picked Kate up in front of the building. Traffic on the South Expressway was slow, and Kate was glad she would not be starting home for a while. Traffic northward to Fulton and the counties beyond, where subdivisions had taken over, would be stop-and-go for a couple of hours. She thought of Jonathon. He had said he would meet her at the cabin after work, but he might have forgotten, and in any case, the time seemed flexible. He didn't know how late she worked—and neither did she. Things were always coming up—such as twenty-five pianos. She looked at Phil Brown, who was intent on the traffic. His blond hair had acquired some gray at the temples since last she saw him.

"Has being a guardian been rough on you?" she asked.

"It wouldn't have been," he said, "except my client thought I was one of dear Papa and Mama's servants and insisted that I dance attendance on her. I spent the last of her money advertising for those nieces she mentioned. In the meantime, the city has some building project going and wants to claim the Bass Street property."

"Not a shrine for the Clay family, I bet," Kate joked.

"You're right." The lawyer smiled sideways at her as he went around a big truck. "Everybody's forgotten that dear Grandpapa was vice mayor during the War and went out with a group of gentlemen to meet the Yankee invaders."

"And plead with the enemy to let Atlanta be an open city," Kate interjected.

"Didn't work, did it? We've been under attack ever since. Look at this part of town. Drugs and crime and poverty have taken it."

Kate had grown up on the edge, the working-class edge, of the neighborhood, and she could remember when this section of town had retained some of its charm. The Victorian houses were getting dilapidated even in her childhood, but the gardens still had the old roses on fences and clambering over caving walls. Almost every yard had a tea-olive tree by its front porch, the creamy fragrant blossoms making of late winter an early spring. Kate had transferred old roses from vacant lots, and clumps of ginger lilies that some matron had probably planted

when Atlanta was trying to heal her wounds from
the War. Now commerce had invaded the neighborhood. Interspersed among the deteriorating houses
were little shops—dry cleaners and liquor stores and
a boarded-up dime store. There had been a grocery
that Kate remembered from childhood as a place of
riches. Children could always get a lagniappe when
they went with their parents to pay a bill. The windows of that store were now covered with plywood,
which in turn was covered with graffiti.

The city, for all its interest in Bass Street, had done
nothing about the kudzu that had pulled down a
lesser house next door and was threatening to engulf
Miss Millicent's three-story gingerbread-trimmed
fortress. Phil took Kate's arm as they climbed the
steep steps to the front porch.

"Watch your heels," he said. "The floor is rotten
and full of holes." They entered a reception room,
which was freezing cold and so dusty Phil started
sneezing and blowing his nose.

"Happens every time I come in here," he said.
Doors led to a parlor on the right. A flight of ram-
shackle stairs led to an upper floor. Kate saw no
chairs or sofas or even tables, but everywhere there
were pianos. Some of them were covered with
sheets. One dead ahead in the parlor had a Spanish
shawl draped over it and its keyboard open and
exposed to the cold and dust.

"Oh, look, Phil!" Kate cried. "A Steinway!"

"There are a couple of them here."

"But so neglected! How could anybody treat a fine
piano so?"

"Same lady who threw rocks at children and cursed the police," said Phil, grinning. "You want to see the rest? There's a Bechstein in the kitchen. She used it to eat on. There are probably sardines and Moon Pies on the keyboard."

"I don't believe I can bear to see." But she followed him through the dining room, where stained-glass windows were obliterated by swags of kudzu, through a butler's pantry, and into a large kitchen with a big black woodstove and a Bechstein grand piano. It was indeed filthy, with old newspapers stuck to its lid and a swatch of greasy oilcloth covering the music rack.

"I'm gon' cry," Kate said.

"Now we come to the uprights." He opened a door to a sizable back room. Vertical pianos of all makes and colors were jammed in there, end to end. Kate pulled her coat tighter and pushed her wool scarf up on her head, winding it around her ears.

"I'm freezing," she said. "Let's go."

"But what about your inheritance?" asked Phil.

"I guess we'll have to let the city bulldoze it with the rest of the house."

"Nope," said Phil. "I got an appraisal from Cecil White, a piano company. They'll bring a thousand or two if you sell the whole mess."

"Spare parts?" suggested Kate.

"That and if the grands are cleaned up, maybe they'll be worth something. Steinways and Bechsteins are very desirable, you know."

While Phil locked the door, Kate stumbled down the steps, feeling that she might cry. Where did Miss

Millicent get all those pianos? And why? The grands, at least, she must have inherited.

There had to have been music in the old house when Miss Millicent was a girl. It was built for parties, for concerts and dancing and banquets served to Atlanta's social elite, not to mention relatives from afar.

"Did you ever learn any more about the nieces?" she asked, as Phil started the car.

"Still got researchers looking in Mississippi," he said.

The lawyer's old Chevy whimpered and gasped, but it moved. Reaching the end of Bass Street, they followed Washington Street to Memorial Drive, and at the corner of the old rock wall that enclosed Oakland Cemetery they turned into a little street of black shotgun houses. Kate remembered one where a peach tree bloomed gloriously in the spring, and she craned her neck to see if it was still there. It was, gaunt and leafless now in the December cold, but apparently still alive behind a rusty hog-wire fence surrounding a hard-packed yard.

Kate felt better. "You know, Philip," she said, "if you can sell those pianos and make any money on them, I'd like to move Miss Millicent's body up to Oakland Cemetery."

"Hmm. That would be expensive," he said.

"More than a thousand dollars?"

"I don't know. Would you want to spend all the money that way?"

"Yes, I would," said Kate. "Miss Millicent should not be buried down there in a public graveyard among strangers. I'm sure her whole family is up here in Oakland. In fact, I bet her grandmother was one of the founders of the Ladies' Memorial Association, which started Oakland as a place to bury the Confederate soldiers killed in the Battle of Atlanta. You know they went out personally, those ladies did, and brought the dead back from the battlefield in buggies or carriages or whatever they had."

"So I've heard, many times. My great-great-grandmother was a founding member."

Kate laughed. "I'm sorry. I forgot you are Old Atlanta. Then you agree it's important to move Miss Millicent."

"I agree," he said, pulling up in front of the newspaper building. "I think you're a great girl to want to do it. I'll get what I can for that junk and call you."

The trip to look at the pianos had taken less than an hour, but the expressway north was still jammed with home-going traffic. Kate wondered if she had a date—if Jonathon would go to the cabin and, not finding her there, leave.

When she was a teenager, having her first dates, usually with a policeman's son, it didn't matter so much if she was late getting home from her after-school jobs. Her father was always there in his wheelchair, jolly and welcoming and no doubt more interesting to the visiting boy than was Kate herself. He had been a hero in the department, had risked his life to save two younger officers, and then had caught a holdup man's bullets in his spine, never to walk again.

But he was vitally interested in life, and poor as they were on a policeman's pension, he taught Kate and her friends the joys of gardening and cooking and, his specialty, collecting sounds on a complicated system of tape recorders. He was fascinating to young men who had thought the high point of their evening would be taking Kate to Lakewood Park to ride on the Ferris wheel or, if they had the use of a car, parking somewhere.

She had never worried if she was delayed in her shopping or if the old bicycle on which she got around Atlanta gave her trouble and she had to push it home. Captain Kincaid was a reliable stand-in to boys waiting for her to arrive. It was he who sold Benjy on Kate. They had despised each other as children attending police outings at Grant Park. Benjy's father, who advanced to superintendent of the traffic bureau, had liked Kate too much for his son to pay attention to her. It wasn't until they were older that he gave Kate any notice. When she and her father solved a killing at the newspaper and she herself barely escaped death, Benjy discovered he was in love with her.

Benjy's career in the department was moving ahead, and he asked Kate to marry him. Captain Kincaid made the wedding cake, and he proudly gave his daughter into the keeping of young Lieutenant Mulcay at a ceremony in the front room of their little house in downtown Atlanta. The Captain's stereo played the wedding march, and a platoon of officers from the department lined up on either side of the front walk to make an aisle through which the bridal couple walked. All they needed was crossed swords, Kate thought, dizzy with happiness to have Benjy's arm around her but worried at leaving her father, who waved merrily from the front porch.

As it turned out, they did not leave him but occupied the room that had been Kate's all her life. The small, squarish clapboard cottage was one of a row of those occupied by tradesmen and artisans who served the owners of the Victorian mansions a few blocks away. Captain Kincaid made it comfortable for them, with hot meals ready to put on the table when Benjy got home from the cop shop and Kate got home from the newspaper office, where she was ecstatically getting experience covering politics and murder trials.

The city had started acquiring blocks of little houses, many of them in the last stages of dilapidation, to clear a parking lot for the new stadium, when Captain Kincaid had a stroke and died in his backyard. A pocket on his wheelchair had been full of peony roots, and Kate often wondered if he had realized that the time had run out for a garden in downtown Atlanta and he had willed himself to die.

By the time the bulldozers were on their street, Kate and Benjy had found the log cabin in the country and were ready to move anyhow.

They might not have bought the old cabin and shored it up if Benjy had realized he was going to die young and leave Kate a widow stranded in the country. He might have worried that she would be alone, but as long as their country neighbors held on against the influx of subdivisions, Kate did not feel

particularly alone. And when young corporate exec-
utives came in, building half-million-dollar houses,
what she felt was estranged.

Of course there were times, she admitted to herself, as she maneuvered her car past the tollhouse on
route 400, when she felt an acute aloneness. The bed
she and Benjy had occupied seemed too big and too
cold. And when she saw couples riding together on
the expressway or shopping together at the super-
market, she felt left out and on the edge of life as
happier people lived it.

She had known nobody could take Benjy's place,
but from time to time she found herself attracted to
men she met. Like this minister ... She stepped
down on the accelerator. She did hope he would be
there when she got home.

Jonathon's old truck was in her driveway, and he
sat on the back steps, her dog, Pepper, stretched out
beside him. There was a light in the kitchen.

"Hi. You have company," Jonathon said.

"You and who else?" asked Kate. "Incidentally, I'm
very glad to see you."

Before Jonathon could answer, the kitchen door
popped open and the Gandy sisters from down the
road, Sheena and Kim Sue, aged thirteen and twelve,
emerged.

"Miss Kate ... Miss Kate!" they cried together.
"We come to git you. Mommer needs you."

"Wait a minute," said Kate, moving by Jonathon
and Pepper to meet the girls and hug them. "Now
tell me what's the matter."

She thought she could guess. Their daddy, who

was prone to drink, had probably wrecked another car or was in the hospital with injuries that would keep him happily unemployed for a time. Sometimes their mother, Lemay, was forced to borrow a little money from Kate, but she was a proud woman and meticulous about paying it back.

"Well, what's wrong? What does your mother need me for?"

"Rape," said Sheena darkly. "Our cousin Sierra was raped."

"Oh, how awful!" Kate cried. "Who did it?"

"That's just it," said Kim Sue, with what Kate felt was a touch of smugness. "Our very own uncle. Mommer's baby brother."

"You heard of him," Sheena said. "He's a musician—the leader of Charlie's Crawdads."

Kate hadn't heard of him, but she assumed he was young—a high school dropout, probably—and very glamorous to members of the family.

"Mommer says it's criminal, what he done, and you being in with the law, you'd know what to do about it. She wants you to come." Kate remembered when the newspaper forbade the use of the word "rape," calling the offense "criminal assault."

She sighed wearily and smiled at Jonathon. "I guess I'll have to go. Do you mind?"

"Not at all. I'll go with you. I happen to have had some experience in these matters."

Kate worried that a man's presence—a minister, at that—might bother the Gandys, but she needn't have worried. Jonathon made himself unobtrusive as he followed her and the girls down the dirt road.

Once in the yard, Kate slowed down, and
Jonathon took her arm. The stuff the Gandys collected—mostly old car parts, but also feed bins and
plows and pulleys hanging from trees, often used to
hoist ailing cars into the air—made walking haz-
ardous. The girls, surefooted on familiar ground,
rushed ahead. Kate was glad to see a plume of smoke
emerging from the chimney. The big railroad-depot
potbellied stove was in service, and it was the right
night for it, windy and chilly after a string of warm
days.

The Gandys' house, once a snug tar-paper-cov-
ered shack, had progressed to a double-wide trailer,
probably when Grandpa's old cornfield was sold to
the subdivision developers. It was a defacement on a
pretty wooded hill, Kate thought, but she could see
why the family was proud of it. Tonight it was tight
and warm, and the front room—with its collection
of lavender and beige armchairs, bought from the
waiting room of the MinuteLube when it changed its
decor to Naugahyde and stainless steel—was downright welcoming.

The occupants of the room were not.

Lemay Gandy, a pretty young woman with a tan-
gle of dark-red hair pulled into a knot on the back of
her head, stood up from a recliner in the corner and
came toward Kate and Jonathon, looking shy and
tongue-tied. She wore a flowered shift and cloth
bedroom shoes, and she appeared uncertain who
they were or why they were there.

Across the room, her twin nieces, Sierra and
Siesta, who apparently were under her wing, sat on

either side of a big youth with shoulder-length black hair, each girl holding one of his hands.

The mad rapist, Kate thought. She introduced Jonathon and herself to the young man, who merely said "Hiya" and did not stand. He looked neither mad nor embarrassed but sat calmly, his long legs, in tight black jeans, stretched out before him. His feet were encased in high-heeled cowboy boots, and a shirt with bright-colored cow-country scenes drooped out of his waistband.

The twins, aptly named, for they were as different from each other as a mountain range and an afternoon nap, slouched beside him on the sofa. They both wore baggy sweatsuits, Sierra's lavender, Siesta's blue, and neither really clean. Sierra had a curtain of stringy yellow hair hanging around her shoulders. Siesta had dark, curly hair pulled back in a ponytail.

Kate waited for somebody to ask them to sit down and finally said to the boy, "How about getting Reverend Craven a chair?" Then, still standing, "You want to tell me about it?" she asked.

"She was took advantage of," said Lemay, nodding toward the twin Sierra. "He done it," nodding at Charlie. "I'm plumb tore up over it, him being my baby brother and them being my nieces."

"I know," said Kate sympathetically, wondering if their relationship was such as to constitute incest. "What can I do?"

"Call the law, I reckon. You know 'em all."

"Have you been examined by a doctor, Sierra?" Kate asked.

The girl shook her head.

"Well, that's the first thing you have to do," Kate said decisively. "We can take you to the Grady Hospital rape clinic."

"Ain't a-going," Sierra said sullenly. "Ain't gon' be looked at."

"Come on, let's go in the bedroom and talk," Kate said.

Sierra lumbered to her feet and followed Kate into the bedroom.

"Now, tell me what he did to you," Kate said, sitting on the side of the bed. "Did he penetrate you?"

"I don't know about that," Sierra said, sitting down beside her. "He took out his doohickey and put it on my laig."

"On your leg?" Kate, the old police reporter, wondered why she had a sense of delicacy, talking to this youngster about rape. "Did he force your legs open and put it between them?"

The girl shook her head. "He would of, but Aunt Lemay come home about that time and he got outa here." She began to cry.

Kate had a sudden inspiration. "You wanted him to have intercourse with you?"

Sierra, sobbing, sprawled on the bed and hid her face in the crook of her arm. "He does with Siesta all the time!" she muttered.

"And you're jealous?"

"Yes'm. I reckon. Wouldn't he have to marry me if he'd of raped me?"

Oh Lordy, Kate sighed to herself. "Look, it's not fair to cry 'rape' and force Charlie to either go to jail or marry you. Rape is a serious offense, serious as murder. Charlie could go to the penitentiary for a long, long time if he had done that. But he didn't, did he?"

"Aunt Lemay come back too soon." She was reporting the destruction of her hopes.

Filled with disgust and impatience, Kate stood up.

"We'll go in there and you'll apologize to Charlie and your aunt. You have created a lot of trouble, and you ought to be ashamed of yourself." Folklore from her own raising surfaced in her mind. "Men don't fall in love with girls who are easy to sleep with. They certainly don't marry them. If you're ever going to have a nice boyfriend, you try to keep yourself"—she paused and fumbled for the word—"pure."

Sierra sat up and wiped her face on a corner of the bedspread.

"And if you're a virgin bride"—Kate realized she was piling cliché on cliché—"when you get married you can wear a beautiful white satin dress."

Sierra was the age to scoff, Kate realized, but she didn't. She looked impressed. In the front room, she said to her aunt, "I made a mistake. Miss Kate said I wasn't raped."

"*You* said you *weren't* raped," Kate corrected her. "I didn't examine you, but you said—"

"Yes'm, I wasn't," Sierra interjected hastily, apparently not willing to tell her aunt she wanted to be raped. "And, Charlie and Siesta," she said, addressing them now, "I'm gon' keep myself pure and be a virgin bride."

"Shit," said Charlie.

"Big deal," said Siesta.

Sierra was not cast down. She went and stood by her aunt, who reached up and took her hand.

"Now, Siesta." Kate turned to the sofa. "You watch out, or you'll be getting a nasty reputation, scorned by boys and girls in your school. You should spend more time on your schoolwork than you're spending. And Charlie, you might keep in mind that these girls are underage. Keep your pants on."

She glanced at Jonathon, who winked and quickly caught himself and assumed a grave ministerial expression. "That's right, young fellow," he said solemnly.

Kim Sue and Sheena did not accompany them back to the log cabin, and in the Gandys' dark yard, Jonathon again took Kate's arm. And at the edge of the yard, he stopped and slid an arm around her shoulders and pulled her closer to him. It was sort of a fraternal gesture, Kate thought, but it felt good—warm against the chilly night air. Then they reached the highway, and he removed his arm and took her hand.

"You did a wonderful job," he said. "I'm proud of you. What amazes me is how you manage to stay so optimistic."

"Well, you know. They were in trouble, and they asked me."

"You forget I'm a south Georgian and I know the Gandys' kind when I see it. No matter what you do to help them, they're going to find trouble. You want to lay a little wager on how soon both girls will be noticeably pregnant?"

"No," said Kate. "No, I don't. They're good people. They just don't know how to cope in today's world."

Kate felt vastly troubled. Her footsteps on the uneven country road were draggy and slow. She had done all she knew to do, and she was surprised that this man of God had all but given up on the girls.

"Well, Reverent," she said flippantly, "let's have a moment of prayer."

"Touché!" Jonathon said, laughing.

Her hand in his didn't feel as good as she had thought. She took it back and stalked ahead angrily.

The light was still on in her kitchen, and she looked around, wondering what, if anything, she could dredge up for supper.

She produced a bottle and two glasses. Jonathon was looking around the room approvingly. "You have a lot of books," he said, surveying the floor-to-ceiling shelves. "They are useful and interesting, I know, but of course they are also cozy and decorative."

"And they help to insulate the room against the wind that blows through the cracks behind them," Kate said sharply.

"And your furniture," Jonathon went on, ignoring the asperity of her tone. "Where did you get this harvest table and the hunt board?"

"Yard sales, auctions. Salvation Army and Goodwill."

"They are beautiful and just right for this room." He cast an appreciative eye on the wall where the bookshelves ended. It was whitewashed rough boards. Kate had hung a big highway department map of Georgia and surrounded it with watercolors

by friends, some good, she knew, and some terrible,
but all dear to her heart.

They had just settled with their wineglasses in
rocking chairs by the fire when they heard a country
"Howdee. Anybody home?" at the back door.

"Oh, that'll be Miss Willie!" cried Kate, getting to
her feet. Jonathon followed her to the kitchen door,
where Miss Willie Wilcox, her neighbor from down
by the creek, stood with a basket in her hand.

"I saw a truck in the yard, and I thought you
might be a-having company," the old lady said, looking carefully at Jonathon.

"Miss Willie, I'm so glad to see you. I want you to
meet our new friend, Reverend Jonathon Craven of
Saint Margaret's Church in Roswell."

"A reverent, huh?" said Miss Willie, her wrinkled
face wreathed in smiles. "Well, that's a change from
them police and newspaper folks you usually have.
I'm glad I brung you some pot likker for the reverent
to eat. You do like pot likker, don't you?" She examined Jonathon's face to make certain of an honest
answer.

"Yes, ma'am, I certainly do!" Jonathon said, taking
one of Miss Willie's wrinkled hands and holding it
in both of his, in an after-church gesture.

"Sit down, Miss Willie," said Kate, pushing a
rocker toward her.

"No, much obliged. I best be a-going home. You
can make a hoecake to go with this, I know," she said,
handing Kate the basket, which held, wrapped in a
clean flour sack, a fruit jar full of the dark-emerald
liquid in which turnip greens had been cooked.

I can do better than that, Kate decided. I'll make little corn cakes. Suddenly it felt good to be cooking something for Jonathon, who walked Miss Willie to the road and came back dusting his hands ostentatiously. "Got rid of another one," he said boyishly. "How many more neighbors you gon' have drop by before we can be alone?"

Kate looked up from sifting cornmeal into a blue crockery bowl. "Just the girls from the church," she said, grinning. "Hettie, Cece, and Toddy."

"Uninvited and unannounced," Jonathon said, raising his dark eyebrows at her.

A while later, they sat by the fire, sipping hot pot likker from cups and eating thin, crisp corn cakes.

"You know," Jonathon offered after a time, "you live well."

"Hmm. Good neighbors," murmured Kate.

"I heard that you saved Miss Willie from going to prison for killing her son."

"She wasn't guilty, and I knew it," Kate said defensively. "I didn't do much beyond holding on with her until things happened to exonerate her."

"You have a weakness for the underdog, I believe."

"I *am* the underdog. At least I guess I used to be. Policemen's children don't have all the advantages. The high school I went to was heavily populated by rich Buckhead girls. They even had sororities in those days. Needless to say, I never got a bid. As for college, I won a scholarship, but my daddy couldn't afford the books and train fare."

"No college?" said Jonathon, reaching for her hand.

"Oh, yes, I had Georgia State, God bless it. You didn't know it before it was a big university with beautiful alabaster buildings up there on Decatur Street. It was the refuge of working students, with an evening program for people like me, with day jobs." She smiled in remembrance. "You should have seen the old building up there on Luckie Street. We called it LSU, for Luckie Street University."

"And you graduated from there?"

"No, not there. About the time I had all the credits I needed, they acquired a big parking garage down near the municipal auditorium, across from Hurt Park. You know the one with the beautiful lighted fountain?"

Jonathon nodded. "So you graduated from a fountain?"

Kate smiled dreamily. "As a matter of fact, that year they held commencement in the park, and that *was* by the fountain. Everything was blooming . . . tulips everywhere."

"And half the police department there to see the Cap'n's daughter triumph?"

"A lot of Papa's friends came—not half the department, of course, but a pretty show of uniforms. I was valedictorian, and Papa was so happy about that. You know, he was a very smart man, and he didn't get to college."

"A lot of us didn't," he said dryly, looking into the fire.

"Not you," Kate protested. "You had to—to be a minister."

"I was exposed to Duke for four years, but I wasn't

serious until I went into the service. Vietnam made me think there was something better than I had learned, so I took the money my mother had saved for me from what I sent her and went to Sewanee. Good old University of the South."

"Theology?"

"That's right—and marriage. I thought I had found what my life was good for. But she wasn't sold, not while I was in school or when I got my first pastorate. She liked it very well when I was an associate at a big church in Virginia and spent a lot of time having tea with rich old ladies, the kind who were a help to her career as an actress. But a poor church with no style—like the one I finally got—was not for her."

"A Catholic friend of mine once said that kind of wife was the best argument he knew for a celibate priesthood."

He laughed. "I wasn't celibate then, and neither was she. We had a dynamic marriage. She got a job in television in Los Angeles, and here I am."

"I'm sorry," said Kate, taking back the hand he had been holding and standing up to poke the fire.

He stood beside her. "Celibacy here is mostly a matter of public relations. I'm free but for the judgmental eyes of the congregation."

The warmth of his big frame as he stood close beside her felt good, but Kate found she didn't like the conversation—the silly wife, the cavalier attitude toward celibacy. He didn't take anything seriously. And she had not liked his attitude toward the Gandys. He was a little better about Miss Willie, but she had come bearing gifts.

"I guess Miss Willie made it home all right," she ventured. "She's very independent, but it's dark out there and the path through the woods is rocky."

"Shall we go see?"

"I'll go," Kate said. "You don't need to. I'll run over after a bit."

"Then I guess I should be heading back home."

"Must you go? Miss Willie would be very pleased to have you visit her, and of course I like your company."

"Do you, Kate?" His beautiful eyes rested on her face with disturbing solemnity. "I had a feeling you've had enough of me and my misspent life."

"I don't know how to judge the spending of a life," Kate said, lifting her eyes to those large gray ones. "I suppose everything depends on how it turns out. Building a church and a new congregation is no small thing. I hope that's going to be a major achievement for you—and a happy one."

He bowed his head and turned away. "Thank you," he murmured, going to the little closet under the stairs and getting his jacket. He brought out one for Kate and held it outstretched.

"It's been a wonderful evening," he said. "I won't go with you to Miss Willie's now. Maybe another time. Good night and thank you."

Kate followed him outside and stood at the edge of the driveway, watching him back out, before she took the path to Miss Willie's. She lifted her hand in farewell and silently intoned her hero Winston Churchill's farewell to Parliament: "To the future!"

As if they had a future, she thought, as she headed

through the Shining Waters subdivision—a real estate man's corruption of the moonshiner's old name for the stream, Shine Creek—and took the woods path on the other side.

Miss Willie sat by her fireplace, piecing together one of her interminable quilts by the light of a kerosene lamp. She had "the electric," as she always explained. But at the end of the day, when she settled by the fireside, she called on the familiar and friendly illumination of the past. The mellow light brought a radiance to her old face and to the gray hair, which was twisted in a tight knot on top of her head.

Pepper, a frequent visitor to Kate's friend, lay by the old lady's feet, which were in what she called her nighttime slippers, knit uppers she made herself and attached to soft leather soles with the help of an awl to bore the holes. The dog raised his head and looked at Kate and flapped his tail in a desultory greeting.

"Pepper told me you was on the way," Miss Willie said. "He heerd you on the path, and he wagged his tail to let me know. He didn't want to be in the way if you was sparking," she added slyly.

"I don't know what you mean. Jonathon's a nice man and I like him, but there's no 'sparking' that I know of."

"'Twouldn't be amiss," said Miss Willie. "You been a widder woman long enough."

Kate sat in a rocker opposite Miss Willie and stared thoughtfully at the oak log that was breaking open like a summertime watermelon to show its red heart.

"Miss Willie, when you say people are sparking, you mean they are thinking about marriage, don't you? Or are they just thinking about going to bed together?"

Miss Willie dropped the quilt square she was working on into her lap. She put her hands to her face, which had turned pink. Kate, watching her, whooped with laughter. "Miss Willie, you're blushing!"

"'Tain't so," said the old lady, picking up her needlework. "The Lord above knows I've lived too long and too hard a life to be shocked. Back in the old days in the mountains, preachers was few and far between, and there was not a lot of giving in marriage. Couples 'took up,' as we called it, and they succored and supported one another for life. But now, Kate, there ain't no sich excuse. He's a preacher, and you are a virtuous woman."

It was a better lecture than Kate had given Sierra.

"You know, I think I'd like a little sparking from Jonathon, but, Miss Willie, what he wants from me is help for his church. They're going to have a festival in the spring to raise money, and he wants me to put my cabin and the yard on tour. What do you think of that?"

"I think we'd better git to work," Miss Willie said with resolution. "I'll hep you. There's lots to be done, lest we be shamed by them big folks from Roswell."

Kate had a sudden inspiration. Why not put Miss Willie's house on the tour? Looking around at the weathered walls with the old iron bed, the washstand, and the wardrobe, she thought that "them big folks from Roswell," whose ancestors were building white-columned mansions while Miss Willie's late husband's grandpa was building a primitive cabin, would be interested indeed. And her yard and vegetable garden were survivors of a period long gone. People paid money to tour the old Tullie Smith farmhouse at the Atlanta Historical Society's elegant spread on Andrews Drive. There they had a barn and animals—and so had Miss Willie. Her milk cow was no more, but there were chickens and ducks and a couple of scrubby old turkeys that followed Miss Willie wherever she went. Her small vegetable patch was always a model of symmetry and productiveness. In her enthusiasm for putting Miss Willie and her old house on tour, Kate forgot all about sparking and being sparked. She would call Jonathon as soon as she got home.

"Splendid of you to call," he said sleepily. "How warming. Baby, it's cold out there"—he quoted the old song—"and to hear your voice . . . !"

"I know it's cold out there," said Kate. "I just got back from Miss Willie's, and I vow there was ice on the path. But I have a suggestion I want to make. Would you rather wait till morning?"

"Never!" he said gallantly. "If you want to talk, I want to hear."

Kate told him all about her idea for making Miss Willie's primitive homestead a part of the tour.

"I might even persuade Miss Willie to demonstrate fireplace cookery," she said. "She has that big black iron range and she loves it, but city visitors are crazy about fireplace cookery."

"That's a splendid idea," said Jonathon. His enthusiasm made her wonder if he was really inter-ested in her or just in the gardens he might make use of. "I know Miss Willie is poor. How much do you think she'd charge?"

"Charge?" Kate's eagerness abated. Miss Willie wasn't poor. As for charging . . . it was for a church, wasn't it? Jonathon didn't begin to understand country people. "Let's talk later," she said coldly, and hung up.

The house was cold when Kate awakened, so cold she put her coat on over her pajamas and her boots on over her bed socks before she went outside to fill the feeding pans for Pepper and Sugar and the vol-unteer cats, and to spread birdseed over the piece of plywood she had tacked to the old sugar maple stump. All the trees in the yard and in the woods beyond wore crystalline tags of ice, like the prettiest and simplest of Christmas ornaments.

Nature does it better than we do, Kate thought, taking her morning tour of the yard. Nothing gaudy about it, but pure and clear little pendants that shone in the early-morning sun like prisms.

As she walked over the yard, she found herself humming and was surprised that the tune was a Christmas carol. It was time, she told herself, for her Christmas shopping. She had decided on much-needed clothes for Kim Sue and Sheena, and she was thinking of getting them Walkmans. Miss Willie was a problem, though. Kate would have loved to give her an electric blanket, but Miss Willie considered her homemade quilts—mostly cotton but one or two made out of such wool scraps as old army uniforms—"a gracious plenty." She might rebel at "sleeping with the electric."

If the day at the office was quiet, Kate might wander out to the stores and see what they were showing for ladies in their eighties. A handbag was one idea she had—a capacious leather one—but Miss Willie might prefer the reticule she had carried for twenty years, despite its cracked and peeling hide.

Lotions and creams and perfumes would do for somebody else, but Miss Willie gathered deertongue in the swamp and lavender out of her own garden to scent her scant wardrobe and the sheets and quilts in her pine Jackson press. As for lotions, it would make as much sense to give them to the jaybird, who was even then gobbling up sunflower seeds on the feeder, as to Miss Willie. He was a gorgeous fellow, the jaybird, and he ran off a lady cardinal and two doves before he finished his meal and went soaring away to the top of a pine tree, screaming raucously at Kate.

She laughed and went indoors to dress for work. She felt so full of Christmas cheer that she considered wearing the new cream wool suit she had bought to wear to Jonathon's church. But it was lightweight for this spree of cold weather, and she decided on heavy wool—a pants suit and a sweater and wool socks in her boots for a start. She would top the costume off with Benjy's pea jacket, which she gave a good brushing, and take along her town shoes and change at the office.

The office wasn't the oasis of peace and order she had hoped for. The security guards in the lobby set the tone for the day.

"Hi, Kate!" said David. "Hear your lady with the big limo has been killed, and they're looking for your street friends."

"No!" cried Kate, rushing for the elevator.

"It's true," said Robin McDonald, the pretty police reporter, who pushed in beside her. "Looks bad for Shag and Warty."

There were three yellow Post-it messages sticking to the face of her computer and one in screaming type on the lighted screen: "CALL CITY DESK. MURDER."

A Post-it said: "Lieutenant Hamrick, homicide, called. Wants to talk."

Which first? Kate asked herself. But her training answered for her. The city editor, of course.

"Miss Mulcay!" Bonny Bonnefeather barked at her as she approached the city desk. "Front and center!"

Bonny was an old-time city editor who came out of retirement whenever Shell Shelnutt was on sick leave or vacation. Having trained in the days of Stanley Walker's book *City Editor* and Lee Tracy's feisty performance in *The Front Page*, Bonny barked at reporters, and when he got their attention he talked to them like they were delinquent children.

He peppered his dialogue with a lot of "beats" and "scoops," the kind of thing Kate hadn't noticed in the profession much lately. She loved Bonny and valued his regard for newspapering and even his archaic clichés.

As she approached the desk he stood up—a tall, lean man with a gaunt, pockmarked face and steel-gray hair, in a crew cut, of course. She normally would have hugged him, but he spun his swivel chair around in an impatient gesture and fixed her with a fierce, accusing eye.

"We are in this one up to our asses. Your street friends, the ones you went to bat for with the VA, the ones this paper even editorialized about, are out there somewhere, probably with bloody hands. I don't know what they did to that lady who tried to help them, but it was fatal. You'd better get on out to the house."

"Yes, sir," said Kate, giving him a mock salute.

Now he hugged her. "Love you, Katie," he said, and sank back into the swivel chair.

Kate paused in her office long enough to get her pea jacket and look up Miss Moon's address in the phone book. She called and left a message on Lieutenant Hamrick's machine: she had returned his call and was on her way to the Moon residence.

Celestine
Sibley

She headed out I-75 with the idea of turning off before she reached the perimeter. An old society editor had once told her that nobody, but nobody, lived beyond the perimeter. Society's folklore decreed that you live within the circular boundaries of the big eight-lane highways which encompassed the city.

She felt certain that Iris Moon would be cognizant of
that rule and would have a house safely inside the
perimeter. She planned to turn off at pretty Mount
Paran, but before she reached it she saw three
apparitions, two men and a dog, walking along the
shoulder of the road.

She pulled over. The day had warmed up enough
for them to shuck their jackets, which Warty carried,
along with the rest of their worldly goods in the two
five-gallon paint buckets. Shag stalked ahead, with
Foodstamp on a leash before him.

Kate opened the back door. "Get in!" she said
peremptorily. That sounds like a citizen's arrest, she
decided, and added more genially, "You do want a
ride, don't you?"

"Yes, ma'am!" the two men said together, and Shag
hurried to boost Foodstamp into the back seat. Warty
arranged the buckets back there and then opened the
front door and got in beside Kate. The three of them
enveloped the car in a wave of heavy perfume.

"Whew!" cried Kate, lowering her window. "You
all smell to high heaven!"

"We know it," said Shag equably. "It's gardenia. We
didn't have time to wash it off."

"You left in a hurry because Miss Moon was
killed?"

"Killed?" said Shag, in what appeared to be honest
astonishment. "She was killed? Miss Moon was
killed?"

"Aw, no," said Warty. "That couldn't be. She was
peart as a jaybird in whistling time all night. Made
us git in that Jacuzzi thing and then rubbed bath oil

all over our nekedness and made Shag git in the bed with her. Rocked the bed like a boat in hurricane wind all night."

"What did *you* do?"

"She had me well took care of—a tray of about six quarts of liquor on her dresser. I took a chair and dove in. Didn't pay no attention to them until the chauffeur come in. He was somewhat pissed off at seeing Shag in bed with Miss Moon. She said, 'Don't worry, Beau-sweetie, your time's a-coming.'"

"So when did you leave?"

"First light," said Shag. "She was making us put Foodstamp outside. Cold as it was. He had found hisself a place on a velvet settee in the parlor, and she had a plumb fit over that."

"Kicked him," put in Warty. "Warn't no need of that. He was a-going out the door all right, but she kicked him with one of them little pointed shoes of hern and really hurt him."

"Ain't nobody kicks Foodstamp," said Shag. "Soon as we could, we got our gear and took off a-walking."

"And I'm sorry to tell you the police think you killed Miss Moon and they're looking for you."

"Good Godamighty," said Shag.

"Which one of them jails they thinking about putting us in?" asked Warty with academic interest. He had been in all kinds—city, county, federal.

"I don't know," Kate said. "I've got to go to the house and see Lieutenant Hamrick. You all can wait in the car, if I can find a good place to hide it. No use letting them get you till we see what really happened and what's to be done."

The house was screened from the road by a high
hedge, and Kate found a niche in it she could back
the car into. Its occupants were well hidden, and the
ten-year-old car looked as if it might have been
abandoned there months ago.

Kate walked up the driveway past two marked
police cars, an unmarked one—Lieutenant Hamrick's
probably—and a van from the state crime lab. The
house was the kind of timber-and-plaster manor
house Atlantans built in the 1920s, many-windowed
and with a slight second-story overhang. A screened
porch was on the side. The entrance stoop was
exposed to the weather and coated with ice. Kate
tried the door beside the carport, and it was opened
by Lieutenant Hamrick, who had known her father
and served with her husband, Benjy. He held out an
arm to draw her to him for a hug, and Kate noted
that he was wearing the same cigar-smoke-smelling
gray flannel suit he had always worn, or a reasonable
facsimile thereof.

"Katie, glad to see you. Maybe you can help us
find those hooligans that did this." He waved
toward a sheet-covered body.

"Tell me what happened," said Kate.

"Looks like she was knocked over the head. She
may have tried to run for the front door but fell over
there. Her maid found her about eight o'clock. Lots
of semen—suggests rape. I don't know for sure.
They're taking the body to a lab."

"It might have been voluntary sex," Kate suggested, thinking of Shag, in his slather of gardenia
bath oil.

"Well, we want your buddies," Hamrick said. "Reckon you can find them?"

"Might," said Kate, "but it's hard to believe they'd kill a woman who was being so kind to them. You know she told me she was going to let them use the little guesthouse in the backyard over Christmas."

"We've checked it out. Apparently they didn't get that far. The maid, named Darlene, said they fed the bums in the kitchen. They were eating roast beef and potatoes when she left for her other job—she also works next door part time. Miss Moon told her to go ahead, not to worry about cleaning up, she and the guests would take care of that."

"Did they?"

"Pretty much."

"Then their fingerprints will be plentiful."

"Old Mulcay," said the detective, patting Kate on the shoulder. "Always in there thinking. We're ahead of you on that. The boys have already found oodles of prints on dishes and knives and forks, even the kitchen table and the sink. They put everything in the dishwasher but fortunately didn't turn it on."

"How about the chauffeur?"

Hamrick looked at the notebook in his hand. "Name of Beau Forrest. Haven't seen him yet. The maid said this is his day off." He listened to the activity overhead, where crime lab experts were probably stripping the bed and collecting drink bottles and glasses.

"Well, you'll find him," Kate said confidently. "And I bet he's the one."

"I'm betting on a couple of bums, which you are

going to find for us. Whenever you spot them, call us, Katie, and we'll pick them up."

Kate walked out to the car, wondering what the penalty was for sheltering criminals. Sheltering? Where? She couldn't keep them in her car. In their innocence, they would probably be willing to go back to their Marietta Street corner, where they would be immediately picked up by the police. The regular church and public shelters wouldn't do. The police would check those right away.

When she pushed her way through the hedge to her car, Kate found the question was moot. Shag and Warty and Foodstamp were not there!

Kate looked for a note and realized she should have known better. She checked for footprints and found they led only a yard or two, where they ran into the paved street. Remembering stories of tracking, she looked for broken twigs and bruised leaves in the hedge. Only the smell of gardenia bath oil remained, and that was confined to the car.

Maybe they had gone in the bushes across the street to relieve themselves. Kate got in the car and waited. Growing impatient, she walked across the street, calling softly, "Shag, Warty—here, Foodstamp! The dog was her best bet. He usually came when she called him. But not today.

Kate started to get back in her car, but she remembered something she hadn't asked Lieutenant Hamrick. She hurried up the driveway and met him on the icy stoop.

"I forgot to ask," she said. "Was anything stolen from Miss Moon?"

"Her maid said some jewelry, a fur coat, and a little grocery money she left in a tea canister for the maid, in case." Kate nodded and started back to her car. To her chagrin, Lieutenant Hamrick walked along with her.

He laughed. "Did you skid into that hole in the bushes, or were you deliberately trying to hide your jalopy?"

"I thought I ought to hide a car this old in such a swanky neighborhood," Kate said.

Hamrick laughed again, but she had a feeling he didn't believe her.

Kate headed for the nearest 7-Eleven, which, if she remembered rightly, was about a mile down the road. She had guessed right. Shag and Warty were sitting outside, eating sardines and crackers. Foodstamp was feasting on a can of meaty dog food. The men didn't seem surprised to see Kate. Nor were they apologetic about not waiting for her. They offered to share their sardines and crackers, but she was able to resist.

"Had to git some food for Foodstamp," Shag explained. "Lot of food in that house, but none of it allowed to a dog."

"Well, I've got to go to work," Kate said. "If you need a ride to town, come on."

Still munching their crackers, they climbed into the car, each of them feeding his last sardine to Foodstamp.

"Have you decided where you want to go and what you want to do?" Kate asked.

"No, ma'am. We was a-hoping that you would tell us," Shag said. "You know like we know that we ain't

kilt nobody, and we shore don't want to fall into the
hands of the law."

"First tell me, did you take anything from Miss
Moon?"

"Tell it like it is, Shag," directed Warty.

Shag laughed in embarrassment. "You know how
ladies do—my mama and grandma did it, and I
expect you do it too. They have a sugar bowl or
something in the kitchen to keep change in. Butter-
and-egg money, they called it, or something to have
on hand if the peddler man come to the door. Miz
Moon had hern in a tea canister."

"And you took it?"

"Oh, no'm, just five dollars apiece. There was
more in the can, but I didn't want to be no thief."

"I told him not to," said Warty virtuously.

"But you went ahead and spent yours on eats,"
Shag pointed out.

"Well, taking ten dollars is stealing," said Kate
implacably. "But that's the least of our worries today.
It's murder I'm worried about. They're going to
accuse you of it if we can't find some other answer,"
Kate said. "It's against the law for me to hide you all
when the police are looking for you. I could get in
bad trouble. But I think I know a place where you'd
be out of sight and almost out of the weather for a
day or two. Do you know Bass Street?"

"Yes, ma'am, know it well," said Shag. "Used to be
a mission down there on Capitol Avenue."

"It's still there," Kate said. "Emmaus House. But I
don't want you to go there. Father Ford has enough
trouble without taking in two people wanted for

murder. This old house I'm thinking about is vacant, except for twenty-five pianos and a cookstove. You might build a fire and stay warm, and I'll bring you some bedding and food. You'll just have to stay out of sight—and keep Foodstamp from showing himself to the neighbors. Take him out after dark and try not to let him bark."

"Is it your house?" Warty asked.

"No. It belonged to an old friend of mine, who is dead now. She left me the pianos, and the city is going to push the house down to make way for a parking lot or something. But I think we'll have a few days—at least until after Christmas. They don't get busy bulldozing places down this close to Christmas, and I do need time to do something about the pianos."

"Sounds first-rate," said Shag.

"Oh, but I forgot. No key. I don't know how I can get you in there," said Kate, pulling over to the curb. It wouldn't do to ask Phil Brown for a key. It would be involving him in her crime of sheltering fugitives. She sighed and pushed her knit cap back on her head.

"This place you're taking us to," said Warty, "needs to be got in without a key?"

"That's right."

"Aw, leave it to me. I can git past most any door or winder. I done two terms for breaking and entering."

"Good," said Kate, but it didn't seem the proper answer. Not only was she sheltering fugitives but now she had started encouraging them in their lives

of crime. She didn't want the neighbors, if any were left on the block, to see her delivering the boys, so she looked for a back way in. One of the charms of that old part of Atlanta was the network of alleys, many of them paved with cobblestones. It was where householders set out their trash cans for pickup. She had walked down many an alley in the spring to pick flowers, fugitives from the dooryards out front. Once, she had covered an alley shoot-out. A poor, sick druggie had holed up in one of the big houses, taking as hostage a Georgia Tech professor he found strolling down the street. When the police arrived, he started taking potshots at them. Nobody was hurt, Kate least of all. She had found a safe observation post behind a battery of garbage cans. The Tech professor seemed exhilarated by the experience and no doubt dined out on the story for years.

She found an entrance to the alley on Dodd Street and turned in, mindful of nails and glass that might mangle her tires. There was a garage back of Miss Millicent's house, and Kate pulled into it gratefully.

"This the lock job?" asked Warty, jumping out of the car. In seconds he was at the back door, doing something to the lock. Kate averted her eyes. She didn't want to see how he did it. It was bad enough to worry about a murder rap without taking on breaking and entering.

In a few minutes, Warty was back, beaming.

"All open," he said. "Miss Kate, that's a purty mansion."

"Used to be," Kate said. "Let's go in and see what we can do with it."

They came along, hauling their buckets and Foodstamp, who wanted to linger in the alley and sniff up the fine earthy smells.

The kitchen door stood open, and the house seemed colder than the out-of-doors. She eyed the big iron range wistfully. It would be wonderful if they could fire that up.

"Miss Kate, these old houses have cellars," said Shag. "Might be some coal left down there. I'll take a look."

"Good," said Kate. "Warty, why don't you look upstairs and see if there's any bedding?"

They both came back in triumph. Shag had an old galvanized bucket full of coal. Warty dragged an armload of musty quilts.

"We in business," gloated Warty as Shag stirred up ashes in the stove and whittled a stray piece of wood for kindling.

Before Kate left, the old stove was beginning to clink encouragingly.

Warty had peeled the greasy newspapers off the Bechstein piano and now he was looking at it with admiration.

"You got you something in this piano," he said. "I knowed one in the Catholic orphanage when I was a child."

"Can you play?"

"Some," he said, turning away indifferently to make a pallet out of the quilts in a corner of the kitchen.

"Well, I'll bring you all something to eat, and then I've got to get to work."

"Could you—would you mind bringing something for Foodstamp?" Shag asked diffidently.

"Of course," Kate said, stooping to pat the big dog, who had sprawled by the back door.

She stopped at the market up on Georgia Avenue and got milk and bread and dog food, then she looked around for something they could eat if the stove didn't work. The pizzas were frozen, but there was a machine with revolving hot dogs cooking in it, so she stocked up on hot dogs and buns.

When she pulled up in the alley, Shag started out the back door to meet her, but she waved him back.

"Stay inside," she hissed as she met him at the steps. "Somebody will see you."

"Oh, I forgot," Shag said. "I got the kitchen so hot I needed a breath of air."

The kitchen *was* wonderfully warm. Coal stirred and broke apart in the old stove, and flames reflected on the dirty wall behind the stove.

Warty was washing something at the sink, and Kate was heartened to see the water had been turned on and there was evidence of domesticity in the little fellow. Miss Millicent had used water from the rain barrel at the corner of the house. But apparently the city waterworks had not cut her off. She had done it herself.

"I found the wrench and turned it on at the street," Warty bragged.

"You stay out of the street," Kate ordered. "Somebody will see you."

"Yes, ma'am." Warty sounded docile, but as she left, Kate feared he was so pleased to be in residence in his "mansion" that he might be sweeping the porch before she was out of sight.

She dragged her mind back to the story Bonny would be expecting from her. She should have asked Lieutenant Hamrick for biographical details on Miss Moon. Who was she? How old? Where from? Did she have any relatives?

She pulled in at a filling station with a telephone sign. Lieutenant Hamrick was not in. She left a message that she had called. Her next-best bet would be Miss Moon's neighbors. With luck, she might find Darlene, the maid, and get some useful information.

When Kate rang the doorbell, she heard the unmistakable hum of a vacuum cleaner in action. She had started to ring again, when the door was opened by a tall, rawboned female in gray coveralls, with a plastic shower cap on her head. She pulled at the cap as she opened the door, disclosing thin reddish hair imprisoned on pink plastic rollers like a collection of uncooked sausages. The shower cap, Kate decided, had been a merciful improvement.

"I'm Kate Mulcay from the *Searchlight*," Kate began sociably. "May I come in and talk to you a little?"

She extended her hand, which the young woman reluctantly took with her own red, rough paw. "I'm Darlene. You want to talk about that air killing?" From her accent, it was apparent that she was from the mountains. Hamrick had told Kate she was young, but he hadn't said she was pretty—and she wasn't. "Pretty ugly and pretty apt to stay that way": Kate quoted one of Miss Willie's sayings to herself. The girl was probably in her twenties, and she had a high-bridged red nose, small eyes, one of which moved up and out independently of the other.

"Anything you can tell me," Kate said.

"Air you a po-leece?"

"Ah, no," said Kate. "Just a reporter, looking for material for a newspaper story."

"I ain't never been in the paper," Darlene said thoughtfully, as if she were considering an appointment to high office. "Let me git Miz Barnett."

"Thank you," Kate said. "I'd like to talk to her too."

Darlene turned back into the house, closing the door behind her. If it was a rebuff, Kate didn't care. She had learned that the neighbor's name was Barnett, and she was glad that getting it had been that easy. If she'd had to ask Hamrick or forage in the red directory street addresses, it would have taken time.

A pretty middle-aged woman with platinum hair and a good figure in her pink running suit came to the door.

"Why, Kate Mulcay, I'm so glad to see you," she said. "We're your devoted readers. I met you once at the Southeastern Flower Show. Remember? I won on roses that year, and you did a nice piece about me."

She motioned to a wicker chair in the sunroom off the hall. "Have a seat. Now, what can I tell you?"

"Oh, everything," said Kate. "I had only a telephone acquaintance with Miss Moon, and I don't know enough about her to write a decent obituary."

"You're good to want to do that," Mrs. Barnett said. "The trouble with most newspapers nowadays is that they just brush off death as if it were nothing—and sometimes the deceased was a great person, a pillar in the community." She paused and smiled ingratiatingly. "Not that Iris Moon was that. She was a good soul in many ways, but not . . . well, you know."

Kate thought she did know: "not one of us." But however common and ordinary, she apparently had money, and she did live inside the perimeter.

"Do you know if she had any relatives? And where she came from?"

"She never mentioned a relative to me except her late father, who ran some kind of mill in Alabama and left her well fixed financially. She lost her beau in World War II and never married, although she seemed attractive to men. There were always callers over there." She smiled again. "And sometimes stayers. My husband is kind of prudish, and he thought we should protest, but I couldn't do that. Let the woman have some pleasure out of life, I said. She didn't bother us, and I didn't want to bother her. She did join the Humane Society, and I thought that was how she got interested in those street people you wrote about. Now I'm not sure. Maybe it was the men themselves."

"Hmm," murmured Kate noncommittally. "Do you know how old she was?"

"Oh, yes. She was sixty. We had the same birth-

day—though I'm younger—and we gave each other
jokey presents. One year it was garbage cans. You
know, the pretty kitchen kind. That was the year
Maynard Jackson was mayor and he had the city buy
every household one or two of those big, big cans
with wheels. Called them Herbie Curbys."

Kate nodded. She remembered Herbie Curbys
and in the country sometimes wished for one, carrying with it the assurance that somebody would pick
up her garbage.

"Now, about last night—did you or Mr. Barnett
hear anything that might relate to Miss Moon's
death?"

"We saw her unload those men and their dog, and
then we didn't hear or see anything until her chauffeur, Beau, drove in. I don't think he stayed long, but
I believe he came back later. I didn't see him, but that
big car of Iris's is pretty distinctive and I think I
heard it in the driveway sometime in the early
morning."

"You do?" Kate couldn't keep the enthusiasm out
of her voice. "Maybe Mr. Barnett heard or saw something?"

"Never. He sleeps like a log. But you should talk to
Darlene. She spent the night in our servants' quar-
ters here, and this morning she went next door and
found the body, poor girl."

"Thank you so much," said Kate. "I'd love to have
a minute with her if I may."

Just then a pretty girl—blond and pink-cheeked,
with her hair pulled into a ponytail—poked her
head into the room. Kate instantly recognized her

from the church and from Jonathon's the previous night.

"Miss Mulcay, this is our niece from Roswell, Hettie," Mrs. Barnett said.

"Is Miss Moon really dead?" the girl asked, a quiver in her voice.

"I'm afraid so," Mrs. Barnett replied. "Now come along, honey, and let Miss Mulcay talk to Darlene." Feels like I can't escape this girl, Kate thought to herself.

Mrs. Barnett and Hettie left the room, and after a moment Darlene reappeared. Kate began by asking her about the slain woman's jewelry.

"Oh, she had some mighty pretty things," Darlene said. "Necklaces and bracelets and rings. She didn't wear them much. Said since the Metropolitan Opera doesn't come to Atlanta anymore, there's hardly any reason to put on all you got. She did enjoy looking at them, though. Kept them in that dresser drawer and tried them on sometimes when she had company coming over or was going out to dinner."

"Are they still there?"

Darlene shook her head.

"Mrs. Barnett told me you spent the night here. Did you hear any comings or goings next door?"

Darlene nodded miserably. "Beau—the driver— he come in twice, but he didn't stay long."

"What was Beau's relationship to Miss Moon?" Kate asked.

By now the girl was red-faced. "Well, sometimes Miss Moon acts like he's her son and she's going to do fine things for him—buy him a car, send him to

college, get him a new suit of clothes. It all depends
on . . . you know."

Kate nodded. "Were Beau and Miss Moon ever . . .
close . . . in that kind of way?"

Darlene nodded. "I think so, ma'am." Now Kate
thought she understood. Beau, tired of her promises,
disgusted by her advances and her promiscuity, had
killed his benefactor in a fit of uncontrollable rage. It
was something for Lieutenant Hamrick. But he
would resist if she told him outright. Meanwhile,
she'd better find Beau and get his version. Heaven
help him.

"Do you know where Beau is right now? I'd like to
talk to him."

"Yesterday I heard him say he was goin' to his
mama's house to put up a Christmas tree for his little brother and sisters."

Oh Lordy, Kate thought. I don't want to accuse
such a family man of murder.

"Thank you, Darlene. This has been very helpful."

On the way out, Kate inspected the plants in Mrs.
Barnett's sunroom. She had trained a bougainvillea
over the front windows, and it was in full luscious
bloom. Oh, for a bougainvillea in her cabin! But it
was too dark and too cold there for such tropical
opulence. Ferns and African violets filled a ledge
along the sunroom's side windows, and the usual
big-leafed house plants, in wonderful clay pots,
occupied the corners. It was not often that Kate was
dissatisfied with her log cabin, but when she saw a
sun-filled room with plants flourishing, she was
almost ready to give up and move back to the city.

Beau's mother lived in an old house in the neighborhood of the Atlanta Federal Penitentiary. A two-family abode, it looked incongruous, one side having been painted pink and the other side blue. Mrs. Forrest occupied the blue side. Kate knocked on the door, and a boy of five or six answered.

"Is your mother at home?"

"Yes, ma'am," said the child. "She's washing clothes out back. I'll git her. You want to come in and look at our Christmas tree?"

"Oh, yes, I'd love to." Kate knew she should wait for an adult to invite her in, but the child took her by a warm, dirty little hand and led her into the living room, where a television set blasted away. The room, like the exterior, was painted blue, with a matching linoleum floor. It was immaculate. Fringed pillows with views of Rock City and Tallulah Gorge stood at attention on the sofa, and artificial flowers filled vases on the mantel, which had been draped with a garland of pine and had three small stockings hanging from it. The Christmas tree was worthy of the little boy's pride—an enormous spruce, it filled the space by the front window and was lavishly decorated with ropes of lights and glass ornaments in silver and gold.

"My, that *is* a tree," Kate said to the boy, who lingered, waiting for appreciation.

"I knowed you'd like it," he said with satisfaction. "I'll git Mama."

He disappeared into the kitchen, and in a

moment a plump woman appeared, her hair tied up and a big apron damp with soap suds enveloping her body. Smiling, she held out a hand to Kate.

Kate started to introduce herself, but the woman stopped her. "I'd know you in a minute—your picture in the paper. It's a pleasure, Miss Mulcay."

"Thank you, Mrs. Forrest. Is your son Beau at home?"

She leaned closer to Kate and whispered, "Gone shopping for the young'uns' Sandy Claus."

"I heard you," cried the little boy. "Beau *is* Santy Claus!"

I can't bear it, Kate thought. I've got to get out of here before I involve Santa Claus in murder.

It was too late. The stretch limo had pulled up in front of the house, and the chauffeur, now dressed in jeans and sweatshirt, was out and unloading big packages.

"Go play in the backyard, Kevin," the woman directed, and surprisingly, the little boy went.

"He knows it's Christmas stuff," she whispered to Kate, "and he's willing to wait. His sisters—they're in school—ain't. They'd be shaking and sniffing and tearing at the paper before he could get it in the house." She laughed and Kate laughed with her, one eye on the young man struggling with packages that were outsized and slippery.

"I'll go hep him," said Mrs. Forrest.

"Me too," said Kate, thinking at the same time that she might be lending assistance to a murderer.

Beau certainly didn't look like a murderer. Kate remembered him as scowling and sullen the day he picked up Shag and Warty. Today he whistled cheerfully and was downright handsome, with his dark hair and smoothly tanned face.

He dropped the packages inside the door and greeted Kate cordially. "The big one is for you, Mama. Miss Mulcay will recognize it."

"For me—to open now?"

"Sure. The weather's so cold you might as well enjoy it as much as you can."

His mother even then was tearing at the box. Kate, who was watching the son, heard her gasp and turned to see her lifting out a mink coat.

"My God, son, what have you done?" cried the woman, even as her hands smoothed the soft, silky fur.

"Miss Moon sent it to you," Beau said, helping her put her pudgy arms into the sleeves.

"Miss Moon is dead. Murdered," Kate said sternly.

"Dead!" Beau gasped. "How can that be so? Was it them beggars?"

Kate shook her head. "They're looking for you."

"For Beau?" cried his mother. "Beau wouldn't do nothing like that. I raised him right. When they took his father off to the federal pen, I made up my mind I'd raise my young'uns in the church, with nary a lawbreaker in the family. Beau, you didn't, did you?" The last came out as a piteous plea.

"Surely not, ma'am," Beau said. "I went back to the house to get rid of them beggars—I knew they were bad news—but I didn't see no one home."

"So you went upstairs and got the coat?" Kate said.

"She promised it to me. And it's Christmas."

"How about her jewelry?"

"That too. She'd been promising it for over a year now. It was time. . . . Show you something." He pulled out a check. "Went to a pawnbroker on Mitchell Street. Didn't really pawn it, though. I sold it outright to a fellow who was in there. Got six thousand dollars for the lot."

"Oh, son," Mrs. Forrest whimpered. "That's stealing."

"Better me than them," he said cheerfully.

"But tell me—why'd she promise it to you?"

"Said I was like a son to her and she had nobody else. That money will finish paying for this house, Mama." He turned to Kate. "Mama's been paying on this house for ten years, hoping to get it paid off by washing and ironing for other folks. This money"— he patted the pocket in which he had replaced the check—"this will clear it up. But I don't know anything about that poor woman's being murdered."

"Oh, son," cried his mother, putting her mink-enwrapped arms around him. "You are the best thing. The law will find you're innocent. Miss Mulcay, will you help us celebrate with a cup of tea?"

Kate didn't feel like celebrating. She felt like crying. But the woman's bright eyes and rosy face persuaded her.

Mrs. Forrest draped the coat on the sofa and hurried to the kitchen. "I give up coffee ten years ago, when I realized just how much mileage you could get out of a tea bag."

"That's my ma," said Beau, smiling proudly at Kate. "Tea's fine, Ma, but tonight you can put on your fur coat and we'll go out to one of them new Starbuck coffeehouses. We'll take the young'uns too, get 'em some ice cream, and they can see Santa Claus while we're out."

Kate drank a really good cup of tea hastily. She had to go. She had to get out of the clean kitchen with its gingham curtains and its abundance of mother-son loving-kindness.

What could she tell Lieutenant Hamrick? Nothing, she decided. Let him find out for himself. Let him see the big Christmas tree and Beau and his mother and his siblings and the mink coat. She didn't buy Beau's story, but she didn't want to dwell on it. He was so good to his family! She headed back to the office.

The story was easy enough to write. Buckhead matron slain in her home, apparently by burglars. Such biographical stuff as she could muster and quotes from Lieutenant Hamrick that no suspects had been arrested. No mention of Shag and Warty, on the theory that if they read the paper and saw that they were suspects, they would disappear into one of the caverns of the homeless by the railroad bridges, even hop a freight car to nowhere. Beau, the dead woman's chauffeur, had been at his mother's house, helping his siblings decorate a Christmas tree, at whose summit he'd affixed an angel—a handsome imported angel, it turned out.

Nobody mentioned the fur coat, and there was nothing said about the jewelry. The pawnbroker, interviewed routinely by the police, didn't feel it necessary to mention Beau's sale of baubles to one of his customers.

Upon Kate's return to the office, she had found three phone messages from Jonathon. She finished the murder story and sent it on its way before she got back to him.

"Hi there," said Jonathon. "I thought I'd never hear your voice again. You've been busy?"

"Very busy," said Kate. "What about you?"

"Well, not too busy to think of something we could do together. What about dinner? I could come to town and pick you up, and we could go somewhere nice. . . ."

"I'd like that," said Kate. "I'm starving. No breakfast or lunch today."

"Then we'll eat early," said Jonathon. "I'll leave here now and pick you up in front of your building in forty-five minutes."

Kate was dimly aware that she had been annoyed with Jonathon about something, but she couldn't think now of what it was. She went to the ladies' lounge to wash her face and brush her teeth and try her hand at some fresh makeup. She used it so seldom, she was insecure about applying rouge and eye shadow. Fortunately, Robin McDonald, the pretty police reporter, came in and took a hand. She had mascara for the eyelashes and blush for the cheeks, and she made Kate sit down and submit to a makeover.

"Have you seen Shag and Warty lately?" Robin asked as she brushed on rosy coloring.

"Saw them before they went out to Miss Moon's," Kate said. "They'd left there when I was at the house this morning."

"It's the opinion of Lieutenant Hamrick that you took them away from that house," the young woman said casually. She worked silently for several minutes.

"Now you're done." Robin looked with pride at her handiwork reflected in the mirror. "You should wear more makeup. It takes years off your looks."

I could use them, Kate thought. She had not had all the years she needed to learn what she wished she knew or to have done what she wanted to do. Books she wanted to read piled up, trips she wanted to take were like Robert Frost's untaken road.

"Thank you, Robin," she said. "I might not aspire to being this gorgeous every day, but I'm glad you've made me look better tonight. I was tired and bedraggled, and I'm going out to dinner."

"Cute man, I hope," said the reporter, applying more lipstick to her own already perfect mouth.

"Well, yes," Kate said uncertainly. She did not think Jonathon was a "cute man," but would this girl? Probably.

The minister was parked at the curb when Kate got downstairs. He looked too elegant for his old truck. Kate had a weakness for the clerical gray suit and reverse collar, and Jonathon wore them well. He smiled a picture-book smile, with beautiful white teeth, glorious gray eyes, and stretched out his arms embracingly as he greeted her and opened the passenger door.

"My, you look stunning tonight," he said, viewing the made-up face. "You must have a heavy date."

"How heavy *are* you?"

"Oh, about one hundred eighty pounds. Might have added to that with Miss Willie's pot likker and your corn cakes. What have you been doing today?"

"Same as you," quipped Kate. "Making pastoral calls."

She didn't want to talk about the murder, to confess to him that she had stashed away the prime suspects, Shag and Warty, in an old house on Bass Street. She was even reluctant to tell him about Beau. She firmly believed the young man was guilty, but the household in the shadow of the federal penitentiary struck at her heart. Jonathon, who already thought she was an irresponsible softie, would make fun of that.

She turned the conversation his way.

"Who did you call on?"

"Vestry meeting this morning. Then I made a visit to Ray Elson, a man who sells kitchen equipment, talked about installing a kitchen at the church. Nice man, but too high."

"No ministerial discount?"

"Well, he did shave a little off the price, I guess. But even so, it's more than we can afford. I might consider waiting until an angel comes along. That often happens, you know. Somebody with a Magic Chef dealership might want to endow the church of their choice with the works."

"You need a Methodist or Baptist layman for that," said Kate. "They are the dealership kind.

Episcopalians and Presbyterians run more to the professions."

"I've found that out, I think."

Jonathon had made a reservation at the City Grill, a handsome newish restaurant in the Hurt Building, one of the most prestigious of the old downtown office towers. Kate had been to the restaurant a time or two, always at the invitation of a well-heeled friend. She remembered having a champagne cocktail at lunchtime once, but she doubted if that was Jonathon's style. In fact, he shouldn't have chosen the City Grill, poor as he was. But since he had, she searched the menu for something moderate in price, settling on a salad and lamb chops.

Jonathon picked a pasta dish, which turned out to be a commanding masterpiece of vegetables and linguini. He had ordered a martini to start and suggested the same for Kate.

"I drank two martinis once," she said, grinning, "and I had to take a taxi home. I'll take a Bloody Mary, on the weak side, please."

"I'll drive you home tonight," Jonathon said. "You can risk a stronger drink if you want to."

Kate shook her head and stayed with the weak Bloody Mary, which wasn't very good, considering the restaurant's reputation. Maybe her word "weak" had thrown them off.

"You can't take me home," she said. "I have my car in town."

"Then I'll follow you home. On second thought, why don't you follow me home? I have some plans for the garden festival I want to show you and a lot

of seeds a friend in the horticulture business sent
me. I'd like you to have them—and share them with
Miss Willie if you think it's appropriate."

"I can stop by for a minute," Kate said. "It's been
such a day I need to get home and go to bed."

He slid a small rectangular package, wrapped in
typewriter paper and secured with twine, across the
table.

"A little present. I'm not good at gift wrapping, as
you can see."

"Looks fine. What is it?" Kate wrapped her fingers
around it.

"Well, I know from reading your past columns
that you are partial to Johnny Mercer. You wrote that
one of your favorite downtown haunts is the little
Mercer Museum at Georgia State. There's a particular Mercer song I want you to hear. You'll find out
when you get home and open this."

Kate tucked the package in her purse, delighted
with him and full of anticipation. She had written
about the Mercer Museum months ago. How did he
know about it? She didn't ask.

They lingered over coffee, and Kate thought of
Beau taking his mama out to a coffeehouse. She
knew she should be hoping that the police would see
him and pick him up, but she wasn't. It would ruin
the outing for Mrs. Forrest, and remembering her
damp and soapy apron and her ten years of trying to
pay for that funky little blue half-house, Kate hoped
instead that Beau wouldn't be taken into custody
until some future, un-Christmasy time.

"Are you going to Valdosta for Christmas?" she

asked. "I mean, after the services at the church?"

"No, I haven't anybody left there anymore. I was hoping you and I might spend the remnants of the day together." He reached across the table for her hand.

Kate felt her cheeks under their layer of makeup flush. "I'm glad," she said. "We'll plan something."

"Now that I'm settled in at the church, I can think about the future. Actually, they could decide not to keep me on. There was mention at the vestry meeting that it would be better if I was safely married to some suitable woman. They said it lightly, but I'm afraid it's serious with at least one member, whose teenage daughter has been"—he paused, looking embarrassed as he sought a tactful word—"has been rather forward."

Kate laughed. "You mean the girls are still flinging themselves at you?"

He nodded. "One of them is particularly aggressive. But I suppose I shouldn't involve you in this."

Kate sipped her coffee and looked at him thoughtfully. "Well, then, I won't ask. Would you mind going somewhere else, if the alternative is having the vestry dictate your private life for you?"

"Yes, I would mind. I have found what I want here—and you are a part of that, Kate. Have you ever thought of marrying again?"

Kate shook her head in surprise. "The question never came up," she said, grinning.

He paid for their meal and left a tip on the table. "It's probably presumptuous of any man to think he can succeed your beloved Benjy and make a place for

himself in your already full life. But I can't believe it isn't possible. Think about it."

Oh my goodness, Kate thought as he drove her to her car. Was that a proposal? If so, do I want it?

Then, as she followed after him, she thought she might. It would be nice to have somebody to go home to.

Before she could get out of the car at Jonathon's little house, she was immobilized by movement inside the house. Jonathon was at the door with his key, when a girl, buck naked, passed between the living room lamp and the windows, headed for the front door. Kate couldn't tell who she was, but the body was young and beautiful.

Jonathon opened the door, and the girl flung herself into his arms.

"Kate," Jonathon called to her. "I'm terribly sorry—" But she didn't stay to hear the rest.

The phone was ringing as Kate reached the back door of her cabin. She didn't answer it. She turned up the thermostat on the furnace and fed Pepper and Sugar before she went upstairs and started undressing. Her handbag on the bed looked fat with the tape Jonathon had given her, and she took it out and turned it this way and that between her fingers.

Did she want to hear it? She did and she didn't. Finally, she put on her warmest robe and her fleece-lined slippers and went downstairs and slipped the tape into the player.

It was an old recording. The first song was Margaret Whiting singing "Too Marvelous for Words."

Before it was over, Kate had started crying. She wasn't wonderful or marvelous. That naked young nymph she had seen in the lighted room was all of that, and Kate didn't blame Jonathon for opening his arms at the front door. Hadn't he done that? She was sure he had. But what else could he do on a cold winter night when someone came to meet him without a stitch on? Kate turned off the tape and went upstairs and put her head down on a pillow and bawled.

When she was exhausted and half asleep, the phone rang again, and out of habit she answered it. She was always afraid of missing fast-breaking news. It was Jonathon.

"You ran out on me," he said. "You should have helped me cope."

"I should?" said Kate coldly. "It seems to me it is peculiarly and exclusively your problem."

"Oh, Kate," he said, and his voice broke. If she didn't know better, she would have thought the man was crying. "I didn't cope very well. It's a very complicated situation."

Oh-oh, Kate thought. He took her to bed. "Well, I don't suppose you threw her out in the cold, dark night without any clothes on."

"No, I couldn't do that. Her parents are out of town, and she's supposed to be spending the night with a friend."

"And you're the friend? Well, congratulations. She's lovely, and it's lovely to be so wanted, isn't it? Good night. I've got to get some sleep."

Celestine
Sibley

She hung up but not before she heard him whisper, "Oh, Kate, I love—"

Who? She didn't care. She wasn't interested. Even now he had a beautiful child in his bed. He didn't say so, but it had to be. He couldn't throw her out or take her home, so . . . Kate turned restlessly.

Around midnight she decided she wasn't going to sleep, and she turned on the light and went downstairs. She thought of playing the tape again and decided against it. Johnny Mercer's repertoire included many of her favorite songs, but suppose Jonathon's tape included "Blues in the Night"?

She couldn't bear even that humorous tuneful indictment.

But ten minutes later, with a glass of sherry in her hand, she had turned on the tape player. "You're just too marvelous, too marvelous for words . . ." She heard the song through to the end, then she threw the tape in the fireplace, where in the morning she would use it to help start a fire.

Kate was awakened at daylight by a knock at the door. She stumbled into her robe and slippers and tottered down the stairs. Jonathon was there, with a basket of pastries and a Thermos of coffee.

"What are you doing here?"

"I've come to explain—and, I suppose, apologize. I want you to know I don't encourage her, but I can't seem to escape her. Last night . . ." His voice broke. "Kate, it was awful. I didn't want her there, but . . ."

For a moment Kate felt a twinge of sympathy for him. "All that beauty and availability . . . ," she said.

"Kate, I was tempted. God help me, I was tempted. I just can't explain."

"No need to ask what you did," Kate murmured on her way to the kitchen to get two plates.

"No, *don't* ask," he said. "I'm ashamed. I'm sorry, Kate. Will you forgive me? I have some lines here written by an old preacher. They apply, Kate, they apply." He recited:

Discouraged in the work of life,
Disheartened by its load,
Shamed by its failures or its fears,
I sink beside the road.
But let me only think of thee
And new heart springs up in me.

"Nice lines," Kate said, "but I don't think they apply to you and me."

"And you didn't like the Johnny Mercer lines either, did you? I saw the tape in your fireplace."

"Yes, I did like them. But with Toddy—it was Toddy, wasn't it?—in your bed, I couldn't believe them."

"Yes, it was Toddy," he said. He did not say whether or not she was in his bed.

They sat quietly for a moment, and then he said, "Kate, I want to be with you."

"You want me to be that 'suitable woman' who can save you from Toddy and the others? No, thank you. I'm sorry, I can't do it."

"Kate," he began piteously, and the pleading eyes in his handsome face tore at her heart.

She put down her coffee cup and stood. "I have to get dressed and go in to town." Upstairs, she thought she heard the door slam as he left.

The little tape, gray with ashes, lay on the hearth when Kate returned downstairs. She picked it up and brushed it off and held it for a few minutes, wishing bleakly that she could believe it. He didn't love her. How could he? She was not pretty or glamorous—or "that old word amorous," as the song had it. She wished . . . she didn't know what she wished. Would she have been a candidate for his bed if she hadn't seen Toddy? She put the tape in the rack with her others and went out to her car. She needed to check on Shag and Warty. They were probably hungry. And she still had Christmas shopping to do.

When she reached the perimeter highway, she thought of Iris Moon, and on a sudden impulse, she decided to go and talk to Mrs. Barnett again. If Iris had as many "callers" as Mrs. Barnett suggested, it was possible, just possible, that one of them had "called" and committed murder. She knew what she was doing: she was looking for a way out for Beau, as well as for Shag and Warty.

Beau had taken the fur coat and the jewelry, but Iris Moon had promised him more than that. Or so he said. It was a flimsy story, but somehow, after seeing him with his mother and his Christmas-proud little brother, she had willed herself to accept it.

Kate pulled up in front of the Barnett house and was walking toward the door when she saw movement behind the shrubbery enclosing Mrs. Barnett's prize rose garden. She changed course and was approaching the rose garden when she heard Hettie's young, well-bred voice, shrill with accusations interrupted by sobs.

Kate's impulse was to go to her side—poor unhappy girl. But then she heard a man's voice, low-pitched and urgent. Beau, she realized, and she stepped behind a big camellia bush, which was dense with green leaves.

"You can't do it, baby," he said urgently. "Stay quiet, say nothing."

"It's not right!" the girl cried.

"Right," said Beau masterfully, "is what I say it is!"

Oh Lordy, Kate sighed, turning away. She didn't know what to make of it, and she hadn't time to puzzle it out.

Lieutenant Hamrick had left a message at the office. She returned his call.

"Katie, do you know where Shag and Warty are?"

Kate had been raised not to lie to the police, so she employed a subterfuge. "I'm not sure," she said. "But I'd think one of the shelters."

"You know they won't take that dog. Besides, the woman who runs that 7-Eleven out on Mount Paran Road seems to think she recognized you as the person who picked the bums up yesterday when they left Miss Moon's."

"Are you going to believe her or me?"

"If you tell me you didn't pick them up, I'll believe you," the lieutenant said.

She tried a diversionary tactic. "You know you're wrong to put the blame on Shag and Warty. They wouldn't kill a flea. Have you found the chauffeur, Beau Forrest? He as good as admitted to me that he was there at the right time, and he may have stolen stuff."

"Know where he might be?"

"Well, he lives at the Moon house. If you all haven't locked him out, he may be there now."

"Okay. And Kate—I'll still talk to you later," Hamrick said, and hung up.

Kate grabbed her coat and hurried to the parking lot. If the police questioned Hettie, she would probably give them Beau's mother's address. On the off chance that Beau was telling the truth, Kate wanted to buy him as much time as possible.

The limo was in front of the Forrest house when Kate arrived. Beau, barefoot and tousled, met her at the door.

"You've got to get rid of that monster out there. It'll draw police like flies. Where does it belong?"

"Aw, it's rented. Miss Moon has—had—a big car, but she loved to rent the stretch kind. I was gon' take it back today."

"Better not," said Kate. "Let's think about that a little. Is there a place around here where you can hide it temporarily?"

He looked doubtful. It would stand out like a sore thumb anywhere in that neighborhood of ancient pickup trucks.

"I know," said Kate. "The Carter Center, the library and museum over on Copenhill Avenue. Dignitaries from all over the world come there, some of them in stretch limos, I'm sure."

Beau grinned. "I'll be ready in a minute. Want me to follow you there?"

"I guess," Kate said. "I want to talk to you when we get there."

The Carter Presidential Center comprised five low-slung white buildings spread out on the second-highest point in Atlanta, a mile from downtown. From that eminence General William Tecumseh Sherman had watched the city burn. Now diplomats attended international peace talks there, and buses brought schoolchildren and tour groups. The former President and his wife maintained an apartment on the second floor of the main building. Kate loved the rolling green hills that encompassed the buildings, the flowering shrubs and trees in season, and the sparkling lake, which, mirror-like, reflected the sky and trees. Neighborhood dogs were known to swim there on summer afternoons, but now a thin crust of ice edged it like a crystal picture frame.

Flags of all the states were flapping in the stiff December breeze as Kate parked in front of the center building—there were few other visitors this early in the day—and waved Beau, in the limousine, to a spot screened by azaleas and camellias. She waited on the walk for him to join her, and suddenly she realized she had brought him into the lair of the secret service.

An athletic young man in the inevitable dark suit and white shirt was walking toward her. He's going to want IDs, she thought frantically. She had hers, all right, having been cleared during the Carter White House years, but what about Beau? She should have known better than to bring a murder suspect into this presidential stronghold.

The blue-suited young man was walking rapidly toward her from one direction, and Beau was coming up the driveway from another. Oh Lordy, save us, save us, Kate wailed to herself.

At that moment the big front door opened, and the former President and his First Lady walked out.

The secret service man paused. Beau did not.

"Good morning," said Jimmy Carter, flashing his trademark toothy smile and extending a hand to Kate, then to her companion. "Glad to see you all."

"And Merry Christmas," said the fair Rosalynn, who too offered her hand.

Kate had not always liked the ex-President, but she adored him now.

"Thank you, ma'am," cried Beau, delightedly rubbing the hand that had been shaken.

The Carters and the secret service man moved on, and Kate and Beau went through the big front door into the lobby, where a pretty white-haired woman

Kate had known for years offered them a tour of the center and the big museum connecting with it.

"As you know, I have seen the center a few times," Kate told her, smiling. "But my young friend here would like the works, particularly the oval office."

"That's in the museum," said the volunteer. "You can ask questions, you know, and President Carter has taped answers for you."

"Goddamn, that's really something," said Beau, still stroking his right hand. "Mama will never believe I met the President and he shook my hand like I was somebody. She purely dotes on that man. The way he got all those habitat houses built for poor folks we know."

"Let's get a cup of coffee," Kate said hastily, eager to get him away from the gentle guide before he revealed more about Mama and their lives.

In the sunny cafeteria, almost empty of visitors, they took coffee to a table by the window. Kate got right to the point.

"I'm gon' have to leave you here until I get a few things done. The secret service is all over the place. You'll see young men with hearing-aid-looking things in their ears—"

"And bulges under their coats," said Beau, grinning.

Kate nodded. "Well, you need to stay out of their way until I get back."

"I want to get to that oval office and ask a few questions," Beau mused.

Looking at the reflected lights of the great Christmas tree that dominated the lobby, Kate thought of Jonathon. She wanted to say to Beau, Ask

one for me: Does he love me at all, or is it some kind
of churchy scam?

Beau had his mind on something else.

"Miss Kate, you think I'm the one that killed Miss
Moon, don't you?"

Kate debated what to say. "Yes, I do," she finally
answered. "Didn't you?"

"Okay," replied the young man, giving her one of
his winning smiles. "Let's have it that way. I got a
proposition. My old man is in the pen, you know, for
killing a federal revenuer. If I'm going down for
killing Miss Moon, why can't I plead guilty for the
revenuer and get Papa a pardon or a parole? That
way there'd be somebody on the outside to hep
Mama and the young'uns."

"Oh my goodness," said Kate, aghast. "They won't
let you do that. It's not true, is it?"

"Yep," said Beau. "I was hepping Papa haul
whiskey. Sold a bunch of Atlanta folks some bad stuff
and made them mighty sick. We didn't know it was
spoilt. It was when I was about fifteen or sixteen.
Short time after that, I was in the back seat of the car
the night a gov'ment man from Alcohol and Tobacco
stopped him. I had Papa's pistol and I used it. It was a
mistake, killing a man over bad liquor, but I didn't
know no better. I done it and I jumped out and run,
leaving Papa to take the rap."

"But you can't prove that," scoffed Kate. "You were a
child. You'll have to have witnesses. It can't be done."

"Miss Kate, it's got to be," said Beau. "I think I got
one witness. A friend of Mama's lived in a house close
to where we was stopped. I run in there and asked her

to keep the gun for me. Then I run out the back door and got home and in bed before the law got there."

"Would she testify to that?"

"Yes, ma'am, I know she would, especially if you talked to her."

"If I talked to her?" cried Kate. "I can't do that."

"I got to do thinking," said Beau, pushing away his coffee cup. "Mama's got the high blood, and she's almost worked herself down. The young'uns need more than she can provide. I been hepping, but if you let me get took in by the police, I can't do it anymore."

"Look," said Kate, desperately. "I'm not in this. Whatever you decide, it's your business. I just thought I'd help you stay out of jail today, but I can't go rounding up witnesses."

"It's got to be," Beau said again. "I'll give myself up and plead guilty if they'll let my old man out. Fix it for me, Miss Kate, please."

"I'll get you to a lawyer. That's all I can do." She stood. "You stay here and try to keep out of sight of the secret service—and of the Atlanta police, if they should get smart and show up out here."

Beau grinned. "I already thought of all that," he said. "The place best to hide, I've always heard, was out in the open. See that ladder and them paint buckets we passed in the hall? Any suspicious characters around, I'll grab me a bucket and brush and climb up on that ladder and start painting."

Kate thought it quaint that he called secret service and policemen "suspicious characters," but she had to admit that the disguise might be an inspired one.

As for Beau's scheme, she didn't like any part of it. In the first place, she didn't believe his story. But if he was noble enough to try to take his father's place in the pen, she wouldn't try to stop him. Let the district attorney dope out the facts. What about Miss Moon, though? Was Beau really capable of murder?

"Look, I'm going to leave now," she said. "I think this is the safest place for you. I'll try to get a lawyer, and I'll be back to get you. There are buses coming and going here, and that might be the safest way for us to travel. Stay put and wait for me."

"Oh, I'll be glad to stay here, Miss Kate. There's a heap I want to see. And it could be President Carter will come back by and maybe speak to me again."

Poor young fool, Kate thought. If he'd had a chance at museums and libraries earlier in his life, he might not be in trouble now. And the same went for his father.

Back in town, she ended up getting the handbag and an assortment of bath oils and cologne for Miss Willie at Macy's. All against her better judgment, but she felt stymied. And the shopping was a welcome—if temporary—distraction. For good measure she threw in a sensible wool plaid scarf and a knitted cap. The girls Sheena and Kim Sue were easy—sweaters, Walkmans, and cosmetics specifically billed for budding teenagers. Passing through the men's department, Kate paused. It was an incongruous purchase, but she heaped incongruity on incongruity by buying Shag and Warty a necktie each.

On her way to Bass Street, she stopped once more at the big Georgia Avenue market. The cooked food was the best bet now. She imagined that Shag's trove of coal in the cellar had long since run out; she would have to look for the successor to the old Atlantic Coal and Ice Company, where she and her father had bought their fuel and summer refrigeration twenty years back. She got bread and milk and coffee and two roasted chickens, canned dog food and a plastic container of potato salad. As a treat, she bought a pumpkin pie, then she added a stack of paper plates and plastic forks.

Shag met her at the back door of the Clay house and hurried down the steps to relieve her of her grocery bags.

"Come in out of the cold," he said hospitably.

"You got it warm in there?"

"Ah, yes, ma'am, there's a coal pile out here in the shed. We real warm."

The big kitchen was almost inviting. They had two single mattresses they had found in the corner of the room, covered with dirty but smoothly tucked in blankets. The sink was clean, and the big piano, stripped of its covering of dirty newspaper, was downright handsome. A cracked vase held a cedar branch from the big tree at the corner of the house, a red plastic ribbon looped over the top.

"A Christmas tree," Kate said, slipping off her coat. "You've got yourselves a Christmas tree."

"Aw, that's Warty's doing," said Shag. "Ain't much,

but he's took a liking to living in a house and having fixings."

Kate looked with compassion at the little man, who had probably never lived in a real house, unless you counted an orphanage—and a jail. She slid her two Christmas packages onto the piano, close to the makeshift Christmas tree.

"Look, Shag," whispered Warty. "Presents. Ain't they purty?"

"Oh, hell, we ain't Christmas Christians," Shag said. "We hiding from the law. What do you hear from the police, Miss Kate?"

"Well, they'd love to see you. But they're on another trail right now. And if you'll just stay out of sight a day or two, they may pass you by."

"Shag keeps looking for the bulls and the bull-dozer," said Warty, giggling at his own pun.

"Well, that ain't as bad as you, hearing pianos all night."

"Do you, Warty?"

He flushed and turned toward the stove, where water boiled in a tin coffee can. "Don't pay no attention to Shag," he said.

Shag was grinning. "He says they are ghost pianos and they play all night."

Kate was interested, but she could see the conversation embarrassed Warty, so she changed the subject. "There are some paper plates there. You can serve your chicken and eat now, if you're hungry. I'll bring you something else for tonight and tomorrow."

Back at the office, Kate settled down to work only

after she had called Phil Brown. He was in court, so she'd have to try again later. Kate wrote a column and answered some mail and returned a batch of phone calls, none from Jonathon. She wouldn't return the call from Lieutenant Hamrick; she felt guilty about deceiving him, of all people. But if she gave him Beau, all neatly tied up in an old murder and ready to confess and plead guilty, wouldn't that appease him?

She tried Phil Brown again. He was still in court. She got the number of the courtroom, pulled on her pea jacket, and headed down Forsyth Street. Young reporters nowadays mostly took the little rapid transit to the capitol and the courthouse. But she remembered it as a pleasant walk when, in rainy or cold weather, she had darted through a battery of five-and-ten-cent stores and an old-fashioned department store with squeaky floors and the smell of rayon underwear and dusting powder near the front door. There had been one store—Cottongim's—on Broad Street, and she would browse there if she had time. They seemed to have *everything,* and they always put a tempting array of plants out front in spring. Once, when the proprietor had caught her staring wistfully at a jar full of peppermint sticks in the front window, he had sent her a fruit jar full of them that afternoon.

Kate had loved covering the courthouse. In her day, the pressroom was a small corner office on the third floor, next door to county police headquarters. She enjoyed trials, and the county police offered plenty of excitement in her days there. The calls they got to the unincorporated areas of the county were almost always colorful, and they'd invite Kate to go along. There was a woman who lived in a chicken house near Adamsville, on the west side of town—a three-hundred-pound woman who reposed in a four-poster bed set on an Oriental rug. Her husband was a respected employee of the state highway department. Kate was summoned as a literary authority, to vouch for the woman's credentials as a poet, when the husband hired a lawyer to fight her commitment to Milledgeville State Hospital for the Insane. Kate's friends from county police broke up when she was asked from the witness stand to read and assess the quality of a poem that began: "Gitchy, gitchy, goo . . . Won't you pitch a little woo?"

Waiting to cross Pryor Street in front of the courthouse, Kate looked up to the third-floor corner window. Who occupied the onetime pressroom now?

Once, the police invited her to go with them to a hog killing in North Fulton County, where a woman had taken a potshot at her husband. His offense was to carry on a flirtation with a fifteen-year-old girl. He seemed to realize it warranted getting shot at and exonerated his wife when the police attempted to book her. Years later, after Kate had moved to the country, she learned that the hog killing and the concomitant shooting had occurred less than a mile from her cabin, at an old house site on one of her favorite walks to the river. The wife had seen her pass by and explained about fifteen-year-olds.

"He had a bad weakness for them," she said. "I was fifteen when he married me. By the time I got old—

twenty it was—he was after that other fifteen-year-old, the one at the hog killing. After he got out of the hospital, he married her." She laughed. "And then *she* got old. When she was twenty, he found another fifteen-year-old."

"And where is he now?" Kate had asked, hoping the supply of nubile fifteen-year-olds had run out on him.

"Oh, he dropped dead on Peachtree Street a few years ago," the ex-wife reported cheerfully. "All of us that had been married to him got together and chipped in the money to bury him."

Kate hoped her pals at county police had kept up with that saga. But where are they now? she wondered, searching the windows of the old gray building for some sign that said FULTON PD.

Phil Brown was presenting his summation in a pollution case when Kate slipped into a third-floor courtroom in a new building that had been annexed to the old a few years earlier. Tacky courtroom, Kate decided, remembering the splendid marble chambers in the original courthouse. They were high-ceilinged rooms with ornate carvings around chandeliers, elaborate marble cornices, and the tall, tall windows that opened out to the sky and trees on Pryor Street. This was a tight, windowless little room, its walls paneled with some kind of shiny wood.

There was such a small gathering in the spectators' section, Kate decided it didn't matter if the courtroom was squinchy and tacky. She took a seat in the back and listened to Phil's address to the jury.

Celestine
Sibley

After Phil finished, with more eloquence than Kate had thought he commanded, the jury retired, and he looked around the courtroom. Seeing her, he lifted a hand in greeting and, after a brief conversation with the lawyer on the other side, walked back and sat beside her.

"Kate," he cried. "You have come to cover this big trial. Does the *New York Times* have somebody here too?"

"Of course," said Kate. "They wouldn't want to miss anything of this magnitude."

Fifteen minutes later, the jury came out. And, apparently moved by Phil's argument, they awarded his clients a handsome settlement. Kate was glad for Phil and gave him a congratulatory hug.

"Come on," he said jauntily, picking up his briefcase and preparing to leave the courtroom with her. "I'll buy you a cup of coffee at the courthouse cafeteria."

The new building was connected to the courthouse Kate had known by a glass bridge and was an architectural and horticultural triumph—a vast atrium with glass walls and winding stairs and a forest of trees, including a splendid stand of full-grown palms beside a small body of water. There was a busy cafeteria, its tables and chairs arranged invitingly under trees that towered to a glass ceiling.

"Get a table," Phil directed, "and I'll bring the coffee. Want something else—a sandwich or a piece of cake?"

Kate shook her head and smiled inwardly. The piece of cake she would ask of Phil would be to get

Beau Forrest stowed away in place of his father in the federal pen.

The lawyer came back with a slice of chocolate layer cake and two coffees, smiling broadly. He really did feel good over the jury verdict, and this was in the nature of a celebration, Kate thought. She hated to spring Beau on him.

"I didn't ask you," said Phil, pulling up a chair. "Have you heard from anybody about buying your pianos?"

"No," said Kate, "but I've been out of the office a lot the last few days. Did you find a customer?"

"I found a man who wants to look them over. You want to meet us there one day this week?"

Kate shook her head emphatically. She'd have to get Shag and Warty out in a hurry.

"Let's wait till after Christmas. I'll call you."

"Meanwhile," said Phil, "what's on your mind?"

"I'm gon' tell you." And she did, all the improbable story of Beau, practically a confessed murderer, and his altruism. "I know it sounds wild, but can you help him?"

Phil Brown listened carefully, nodding now and then and not interrupting. "I don't know," he said finally. "But I can try."

"Oh, bless you. You want to see him today? I can bring him to your office."

Beau had had a wonderful day. Kate found him in the gift shop next to the Carter Museum. He had bought presents for his mother and the children, and he was in cheerful, animated conversation with Kate's friend Miss Emma, the guide.

"Kate, I'm gon' keep your young friend here," the gentlewoman said. "He has helped me greet schoolchildren all day. His enthusiasm is so infectious."

Beau nodded in complacent agreement. "I want to show you something, Miss Kate," he said. He led the way toward the Cecil B. Day Chapel, a magnificent room endowed by the widow of the Days Inn founder.

"People give these to President Carter," he explained to Kate, pointing out pictures on the corridor walls. "If it's worth less than a hundred and fifty dollars, he can keep it. Otherwise he has to return it. But this one . . . I want you to see it."

He stopped in front of an oil painting showing a lot of people on the deck of a ship. Some of them were crying, some embracing, and all their faces were turned to the Statue of Liberty in the distance.

"They're immigrants," Beau explained. "Look at their faces. They are *so* happy. Just look."

Kate examined the picture carefully, and she was as touched by the faces of the immigrants as Beau was. They don't know, she thought, that they are going to have a hard time in this country. They may be hungry and sick and homeless, but then, if they make it . . . Oh, some of them will make it.

She looked at Beau. His handsome tanned face was crumpled with emotion. "My folks come like that," he said. "Did yours?"

Kate nodded tearily. "I don't know much about

them, but they had to have come . . . from some-where."

"And they made it," decided Beau. "I want my lit-tle brother and sisters to see that picture and to know that they can make good in this country. I reckon they have to have an education first—huh, Miss Kate?"

"And the will to work," said Kate. "Oh, Beau, you could . . . why did you have to be in this trouble?"

He shook his head, in obvious distress. "I don't know. I told her . . . well, it just happened, Miss Kate."

Kate wondered what he meant. "Come on," she said, wiping her eyes. "I've got a lawyer for you. We're going to meet him in his office."

"The limo," said Beau. "What about it? I saw some of them secret services out there going over it."

Kate's spirits sagged. One more dilemma.

"They'll trace it to Miss Moon," Beau said. "And then to me?"

"Probably," said Kate. "Come on. Let's get out of here."

Kate had meant to put Beau on a MARTA bus, but in view of the secret service men's interest in the limo and the virtual certainty that it would lead to Beau, she decided to take him to town in her car—as fast as possible.

They had paused at the stop sign by the exit from Carter Center, when a police car drew up beside them.

Lieutenant Hamrick, riding with a uniformed officer, rolled down the window and grinned at Kate.

"Okay," he said. "You've been avoiding me. Where are they?"

"Where's who?" asked Kate blankly.

"You know, your scroungy friends. They're wanted for murder, Kate."

He didn't seem to be taking an interest in Beau, who slumped beside her, his baseball cap pulled low on his forehead.

"Have you tried Marietta Street?" she asked.

"Of course we have—and every other corner and hidey-hole in Atlanta. I think you know something, and you'd better tell me, Kate."

Kate nodded humbly. "I do and I will. Not now, but meet me at the station tonight and"—she paused and made a comical face—"I'll confess."

Lieutenant Hamrick looked stern. "If you fail to come through, Kate, I'll have to book you for obstructing justice. And as you're well aware, you can't hide from me."

Kate nodded, and he signaled the driver to move on.

"Godamighty," whispered Beau. "He's after *you,* and *you* ain't killed nobody. . . . Or have you?"

Kate smiled weakly. "Not yet."

The only thing wrong with the magnificent Candler Building, where Philip Brown, with his unwavering appreciation for Old Atlanta, had his office, was the lack of parking spaces. Kate finally decided to pull in at Macy's garage, a block away, and walk Beau past the library on Margaret Mitchell Square, where there was likely to be a policeman on duty. There was one, but his attention was on the heavy homeward traffic, which met and meshed where Forsyth and Broad streets converged into Peachtree. She led Beau across the street as swiftly as seemed unnoticeable and into the grand lobby of Atlanta's first skyscraper. Asa Candler, the son of the Coca-Cola magnate, had built it in 1906 to show Papa, he once told Kate, that although he drank whiskey and played the accordion in the Shrine band, he was not a wastrel son.

"Papa said, 'Build me a building,'" the old man had told Kate when she was a young reporter, "and this is it."

To its credit, Atlanta had not changed or torn down Asa's showpiece. The lobby was dominated by a great curving stairway with niches and friezes honoring everybody from Asa's parents to Beethoven and Admiral Dewey, hero of the Spanish-American War. Kate had always heard that on opening day, all Atlanta dressed up and went to town to inspect the building, with children exuberantly riding to the top floor in the elevator and walking down seventeen flights of white marble steps.

There was a lingering expression, "as tall as the Candler Building," even after much taller buildings were reaching for the sky all around it. The building had housed all the important law firms and many doctors' offices until recent years, when real skyscrapers began to go up like mushrooms all the way out the expressways to Buckhead and beyond.

In contrast to the lobby and the hall, Phil Brown's

office was a plain boxy room featuring a rolltop desk that had doubtless belonged to his father. Its austerity was redeemed by a view of Woodruff Park beyond the windows.

Phil, still euphoric over his win at the courthouse, greeted them cordially. His secretary, if any, had gone for the day, and the door to his private office stood open and welcoming. He kissed Kate on the cheek— to her astonishment—and shook Beau's hand.

"Now tell me, sir," he said with old-fashioned courtesy, "how can I help you?"

Beau related the story of the killing of the revenue agent and told Phil that in exchange for his father's freedom he would confess to that and to the killing of Miss Moon.

"If I might ask," said Phil diffidently, "why do you want to face possible death or life imprisonment?"

Beau gulped. "Death? Would I git that?"

"You could," the lawyer said. "It's not likely if you confess, but it's a possibility."

Beau sighed and looked at Kate. "You tell him, Miss Kate," he pleaded.

Kate straightened her shoulders against the back of the Windsor rocker that served as one of Phil's client chairs, and she took a deep breath. "Beau is concerned about his mother and brother and sisters," she said faintly. "He thinks if he takes his father's place in jail, his father will get out and support the family. His mother isn't well, and the children are young. She has worked very hard to make a home for them and . . ." She couldn't go on. She couldn't tell Phil that Beau had stolen Miss Moon's jewelry and sold it to pay off the mortgage on the shabby blue house his mother had struggled to buy. A killer was one thing, but a thief . . . maybe Phil was choosy about that.

Kate had been looking at Beau's face as she talked, and she was suddenly convinced that he was not guilty of Iris Moon's murder. Why in the world would he have killed his benefactor?

Phil pulled out a lawbook and leafed about in it. Finally, he turned around in his swivel chair and cleared his throat. "The first thing," he said, "is that you better surrender to the police."

Kate shrugged. "I thought of that. In fact, I told Lieutenant Hamrick I'd meet him at the station tonight. I was going to take Beau in."

"I'll go with you," said Phil. "And then we'll tackle the federal charge. That may be more difficult."

"That's the only way I'll go in willingly," said Beau. "I got to be sure Mama and the young'uns is took care of."

"We'll do the best we can," Phil promised. "I know the DA pretty well. I'll talk to him tonight. But it's better if you're not a fugitive."

"Well, on the way, can I go by the house and see Mama and the young'uns one more time? I got a package for them from the Carter Center in Miss Kate's car. I'd like to give them that and—you know—wish them Merry Christmas."

"We can do that, can't we, Mr. Brown?" She had been addressing Phil formally.

He nodded and reached for his jacket, which was on a coatrack in the corner.

Celestine
Sibley

The Forrests were all ecstatic to see Beau. The tidy little house was fragrant with something Kate couldn't quite place; it smelled vaguely like something Miss Willie might have cooked.

"What is that wonderful aroma?" she asked when the introductions had been made and the children were swinging on Beau's arms and clasping him around the legs.

"Oh, that's my tater pone," said Mrs. Forrest, pleased. "My mama and grandmama always made it for Christmas. We couldn't afford the makings for fruitcake. But sweet potatoes were plentiful and cheap, and you most always had the spices."

"Mama . . . ," Beau began, squatting on the floor and gathering the three children in his arms. "I gotta go." He jerked his head in the direction of the big Atlanta penitentiary. "I come to tell you goodbye."

"No, son," cried Mrs. Forrest in anguish. "You ain't done nothing. I know you ain't. I cain't give you up."

"Mama, Papa's gon' git out when I git in, so it'll be somebody here to hep you. Mama, it's the right thing to do—and I know you believe in right."

"I don't know what I believe in!" Beau's mother burst into tears.

Kate put an arm around the heavy shoulders in their frayed and faded man's sweater, and Mrs. Forrest leaned against her, sobbing.

Phil Brown, looking miserable, moved one of the fringed scenic sofa pillows and sat down.

"I come to bring you these presents from the Carter Center, Mama," said Beau. "You'd like it there. I met him. The President. He shook my hand, and his wife told me Merry Christmas."

"Oh, son," breathed Mrs. Forrest in awe. "I'd give a purty to meet that man. He'd hep us, I know."

"Not in this, Mama. I done violations too sore and heavy for him to mix in. But it's gon' be all right, you'll see."

He looked at Phil Brown for confirmation.

The lawyer was the picture of uncertainty and pain. He didn't confirm or deny. Instead he said, "Forrest, if you want to take a bag, you'd better get it."

"Yeah," said Beau. "Toothbrush and shaving stuff and some clean clothes. Okay, Mama?"

"I'll git 'em," his mother said, as if she couldn't bear to forgo this last service for him. "Whilst I do that, reckon you could make a pot of tea and serve some of the tater pone? It's done, I know."

Kate was ashamed to admit it, but she wanted some of that wonderful-smelling pone, and when one of the girls brought it in, she reached eagerly for a slice. Phil seemed hungry too, and they appeared oddly festive and contented as they sat by the lighted Christmas tree, eating and drinking.

His family followed Beau out to the car and hugged him repeatedly.

Celestine Sibley

The city jail, like all the institutions Kate had known and covered as a reporter in years past, had turned stately—the new building was tall and white, to match the academic architecture of Georgia State University, which surrounded it. Kate felt at odds with lobby and receptionist and elevators. The police station and jail she had been familiar with were contained in a big, ugly open building with a wide central hall that smelled of motor oil and tobacco spit. The pressroom had been toward the end, and across from it was the desk sergeant, with benches for the people he was booking. Within calling distance was an old newspaper photographer friend of Kate's, who had hooked up with the police department to take ID pictures of the newly booked.

She had of course been to the new-model police department off and on during the years, but she never got over its strangeness. Sometimes she wondered if, more than the humanity, the old friends, she missed the fragrance of Decatur Street itself—peanuts parching in a sidewalk machine, pork chops and catfish frying in the greasy eateries up and down the avenue. Even bananas. Once, she had been there to interview a gentle little woman who had been arrested for a trunk murder, and asked, "Is there anything I can get for you?" The old lady, sitting on a bunk in her cell, with her ankles primly crossed and her straight-brimmed straw sailor sitting squarely on her head, had said, "Oh, honey, could you please, ma'am, bring me some bananas?" Kate had hurried to a fruit stand across the street and bought a dozen bananas, which she fed the prisoner through the bars, one at a time, as she elicited the story of the slaying of a beautiful young woman.

Now there was no peanut roaster, no fruit stand across the street, and she was bringing the prisoner with her.

Phil Brown spoke to the person behind a counter at the end of the hall, and they were asked to wait a few minutes for Lieutenant Hamrick, who expected them.

He came out in his shirtsleeves, his dark tie askew; there were deep circles under his eyes. The lieutenant greeted them without smiling, saying merely, "Kate ... Counselor ..." and aiming a questioning look at Beau.

"Beau Forrest, Lieutenant," Kate said hastily. "He was Miss Moon's chauffeur. Mr. Brown is his attorney. He will tell you the situation."

"Good. . . . Come on back." The lieutenant led the way to an office around the corner of the big booking room.

There was a scarred golden-oak table in the middle of the room, and an assortment of round black chairs. Kate thought she recognized them from years of police interrogations and capitol committee meetings in the days before cigarettes were banned in all public buildings. The dark burn scars were there, the lame legs on chairs that had accommodated generations of overweight public servants.

"Lieutenant," began Phil Brown before they were all seated at the table, "Mr. Forrest here wants to make a confession."

"Good," said the officer, picking up the phone. "I'll get a witness and a stenographer. Kate"—turning to her—"do you mind being excused?"

"But why?" Kate asked. "I brought him in, you know."

"Fine," the policeman said. "Now you may go. We'll call you."

Kate stood up. She really didn't mind skipping the confession. She had heard it all before, and she was very tired. She just hated Lieutenant Hamrick's effrontery in banishing her. Beau reached for her hand.

"Thank you, Miss Kate," he said. "Would you kindly keep check on Mama?"

"I'll be glad to, Beau." She closed the door softly as she left.

Kate was about to drive into the newspaper's parking lot, when she remembered that she had promised Shag and Warty more food. She took the back way along the railroad tracks and under the bridges, toward the southern part of town. With care, she would avoid Underground Atlanta, which she didn't much like. Its restaurants and shops catered to tourists, who swarmed there by the busload.

She, who loved carnivals and fairs, could not explain why she didn't like the Underground development, built on the site of the streets that ran along the railroad before the big overpasses had come along to cover them. There were many handsome facades and doorways surviving, and the shops and restaurants certainly gave visitors something to do when they were in a downtown area largely stripped of its stores. The only answer she could think of was that, like malls and subdivisions, it was unnatural. It had grown not out of need but out of promotion.

She surfaced on Butler Street and headed toward Georgia Avenue and the big market. It wasn't the most prestigious market in town, didn't cater to gourmet cooks and offer up exotic pâtés and a glorious array of fresh vegetables and meats and ethnic breads. But it had basic victuals, Kate decided, and whom was she shopping for except homeless beggars?

With Christmas in mind, she bought half a cooked turkey and dressing, a small fruitcake, and milk and eggs and bread. The store gave away bones, and she examined these carefully, noting enough meat on them to make good soup. Kate got two, one for Foodstamp and the other in case Shag and Warty had found a big pot. She considered buying one in the kitchenware section, then remembered that the prospective piano buyer might be on the way soon and they would have to get out of the house, taking their gear with them. There was no use adding one more thing to the stuff they hauled around in their buckets. Kate completed her shopping with an onion, potatoes, canned tomatoes, apples, oranges, and two big peppermint sticks.

The sun was sinking beyond the big new stadium when Kate pulled into the alley back of the house on Bass Street. A robust tendril of smoke flowed out of the kitchen chimney into the icy December twilight, and Kate was thankful once again that the neighbor-

hood was so far gone that there were no neighbors to see it and wonder.

Foodstamp barked a proprietary, at-home bark as Kate climbed the back steps, and Warty pressed his face against the window glass to check. She heard him yell, "It's Miss Kate, Shag! She's bringing stuff." And then both of them were out the door and reaching for the grocery bags.

The kitchen had been scrubbed, and so, decided Kate, had its occupants. There was a functioning bathroom, they said, but it was on the second floor and so cold they filled their buckets and bathed by the kitchen stove.

"Well, you look nice," Kate approved. "And I think I have some good news. Beau Forrest, the chauffeur, even now is telling the police that he killed Miss Moon. If they charge him and lock him up, you all should be free."

"Oh, I know Beau-sweetie was mad with jealousy agin me," said Shag, "but I didn't think he was killing mad."

Kate sighed. "I don't know. If he says he did it, that will probably be enough for the police. I think you all are safe here till Christmas, but not long after that a man is coming to look at the pianos, so you'll have to clear out."

"You selling 'em?" asked Warty.

"If anybody will have them."

"The Bechstein too?"

"I guess so. I don't know anything about it, but if it's worth buying, I've already got a use for the money."

Warty ducked his head and laid a scarred, shriveled hand on the Bechstein's cover. "Fine piano," he said.

"Is it?" Kate asked. "We had an upright at home—a Baldwin, I think. And there was a Steinway in the Sunday school room at the church. But these here must be pretty well shot by now."

"Yeah," said Warty morosely. He returned to unpacking the bags Kate had brought.

"Well," echoed Kate. "I'd better go."

"We was wishing we could invite you for Christmas," Shag said. "Don't seem right, with you bringing all the groceries. But it'll make the day for us to have your company."

"If I can, I will," Kate said. "And thank you."

She headed out Northside Drive toward the expressway. At I-75, she would slip into 85 and with luck be on 400 and homeward bound in moments. She hated the lane-changing, and she was always uneasy about getting on the toll road, 400, until she had made sure she had the correct fifty cents. They would change currency, but she had a feeling it inconvenienced them to change more than a dollar, so she tried to go prepared.

The upside of it was that as soon as she had deposited her fifty cents in the tollhouse's big plastic bin, the barrier lifted and a light went on that said THANK YOU. Kate was embarrassed to admit that it always made her feel like a welcome traveler on the state's road. Benjy had kidded her about getting a lift from a toll road sign, but she couldn't help it, it was a reliable achievement, however unachieving her day.

She drove into the yard, to find the Gandy sisters
sitting on her back porch, huddled against the cold
north wind under a quilt.

"My gracious! You'll freeze to death out here," she
cried. "Get on in the house and I'll turn up the heat."

"We didn't want to . . . ," began Sheena. If she says
"intrude," I'll choke, thought Kate. They always
intruded. They didn't call it that, but it was their
modus operandi. They almost always were where
they weren't supposed to be.

She pushed them in ahead of her and turned up
the thermostat.

"Want us to build a fire?" asked Kim Sue.

"What is this?" Kate demanded. "What are you up
to, coming over here and waiting and then offering
to build a fire?"

"Well, we thought we'd keep you from being lonesome," Sheena said.

"Lonesome?" repeated Kate. "I'm not lonesome.
What are you talking about?"

"Mommer said—" Sheena began, then stopped.

"What did Mommer say?"

"That preacher man come by in his brand-new
car. Had him a young girl from Roswell. Me and Kim
Sue said, 'What do you reckon, him coming like that
with a girl in the car?' We thought he wanted to be
your feller. We asked Mommer if you'd put up with
him, and she said you was lonesome."

Kate started laughing so hard she had to sit down.
"So you came to keep me company?" She reached
out an arm and drew them close. "You are dear
friends, and I love you. I might be lonesome if I

didn't have you. Go ahead and build a fire, Kim Sue, and you, Sheena, put on some music while I change my clothes. There's soup in the freezer and a pecan pie. We'll feast."

They sat at the kitchen table, and in the warm glow of the old tin grocery store light, the freckled faces of the girls had a kind of radiance. Sometimes they could be enchanting, as now when they wanted to save her from the "preacher man" by offering their own stellar companionship.

"Tell me about Mr. Craven's car," she invited over the pecan pie.

"Blue," said Kim Sue.

"'Twas not," said Sheena. "It's the new shade of green they're putting on everything now."

"Is it pretty?" Kate got around the subject of color.

"Oh, yes!" breathed Kim Sue. "You'd love to take a ride in it."

"You said he had somebody with him."

"Oh, yeah, a curly-headed girl that goes to Roswell High. She's a senior, I think. Maybe a cheerleader."

"My," said Kate, as if impressed.

The music Sheena had started came to a stop. Kim Sue changed tapes, and Johnny Mercer's "Too Marvelous" poured out.

Kate stood up. I've had enough, she thought. I can't take that. "Let's change the tape," she said. "And then we'll clear away the dishes and I'll walk you all home."

"You don't need to," Kim Sue said. "We ain't scared. It's only a little piece. We want to show you the pitcher we took with that Kodak you give us."

"Later," Kate said, hugging her. "I need to get out in the air for a little."

Kate saw the girls safely to their parents' double-wide and turned back down the hill. The night was dark, but the wind had subsided and the stars were so big and bright Kate paused on the path to look at them. She remembered some lines from Psalms: "He healeth the broken in heart, and bindeth up their wounds. He telleth the number of stars; He calleth them all by their names."

My heart isn't broken, she thought, or is it? If she weren't so tired, she'd be angry and outraged that he had brought his little floozy to her house. Showing off, she thought. Showing the new car and the girl. And I liked the old beat-up truck better. I liked being the one he wanted to marry. Would I have married him? Am I that lonesome?

Kate went to bed, and to keep from crying, she read Emerson for an hour. Both Phil Brown and Lieutenant Hamrick called with the news that Beau had been booked in the county jail on suspicion of murder. She thought one of them was calling back when the phone rang near midnight, so she answered it.

It was Jonathon. "Are you coming to church Sunday?" he asked. "I'm preaching on forgiveness."

"Congratulations on the new car," Kate said. "I hear it is very elegant."

"Yes, it is," Jonathon said, "but I'm not keeping it. It was a gift from the vestry."

"I understand," murmured Kate. "Toddy's father is the big man on that board, and he threw in his daughter as part of the deal."

"Kate ...," Jonathon said reproachfully. "Mr. Dickson did vote for me to have the car, but as for his daughter, she hid in the back seat and did not pop up until we were halfway to your house. I didn't turn back, Kate, because I thought you would be big enough to see the humor in it and would understand."

"I think I understand," Kate said. "Good night."

"Kate! Kate!" he called. "Please don't hang up. Listen to me!"

"I don't want to listen," Kate said. "I want to go back to sleep. If you pray for forgiveness in your sermon tomorrow, you can throw my name in the pot. I can use a lot of it."

Sleep eluded her. She got up and poked at the fire and put another log on. She considered a glass of sherry and finally decided on a cup of cocoa. Sugar and Pepper found spots with the sofa to their backs and Kate's feet and legs as a buffer to the fire when it got too hot.

"Lazybones," she murmured, stroking first one and then the other. It reminded her of Jonathon's gift. Mercer also wrote "Lazybones." She had known Jonathon too short a time to have things keep reminding her of him.

She didn't know why the idea of him in a new car offended her so. It stood to reason that a nice Episcopal congregation would not want their rector riding around in a disreputable vehicle. She may have been wrong to assume that Toddy Dickson's father was the prime mover in the car deal, that he was trying to buy Jonathon for Toddy. She pulled up the

Celestine
Sibley

wedding ring quilt she kept on the back of the sofa
and finally went to sleep there, with her clothes on.

The telephone awakened her at six o'clock. A
young female voice was screeching: "Miss Kate, Miss
Kate, come and git me!"

"Who is this?" mumbled Kate foggily. "Where are
you?"

"It's Sierra. I'm in jail!"

"Which jail? Why?"

"Fulton County Jail," said a woman's voice. "Rice
Street."

Kate's questions were cut off by a third voice: "Tell
Tawanda to git out the shower and talk to me."

"Hello ... hello?" pleaded Kate. "Somebody
answer."

The line went dead.

The jail Kate had known well was the old Fulton
Tower, downtown. She visited it often and regretted
when Fulton County and crime had both bur-
geoned and it was necessary to build a new jail out
west of town, on a sprawling piece of country
acreage off the Bankhead Highway. She had heard
that the new jail, a massive structure of brick, was
modern in every way, including the new-style
crimes of its denizens, crimes of drugs and child
abuse, crimes that were barely known of in the days
of the Fulton Tower. One of her favorite memories
of the tower involved a gentle, courtly white-haired
man, the member of an old Atlanta family, who was
incarcerated for murder.

He had shot a gambler who was looking for him
at the Ansley Hotel, a gun in his hand. The coroner's

jury held that it was self-defense, and he would have been released, had it not been for his family's political opposition to the prosecuting attorney. Allowed out on bail before he was brought to trial, he took off for the West, and twenty years later a postal inspector saw him on a Los Angeles golf course, recognized him, and returned him to Georgia for trial. He was convicted and sentenced to life.

Kate was sent to interview him when he attempted suicide. She remembered the tower as being clean and nearly empty, and he was in a cell on a floor by himself. He didn't want to be interviewed but was too courteous and old-fashioned to refuse a young woman when she asked him shyly for permission. He had been reading a letter, and he offered it to her.

It was from his wife, who lived in a small town in California. She had been informed that he was in the hospital—but not given the reason. She expressed worry that he was ill and wished that she could have been with him, to sleep on a cot beside his bed, "as we always do when one of us is sick." She said a man had come to give her an estimate on a new roof, spoke of their little girl's performance in the children's choir at their church, and ended, "The roses are doing so well this year. I wish that you were here to see them."

Kate looked up from the handwritten letter, her eyes brimming. A cot beside a hospital bed, the roof, a child's choir practice, roses . . . P.S. I love you. A letter so normal and wifely, so loving . . . This man could not deserve to be in jail!

The story she wrote did not get him out of jail,

but it wasn't many months before her continuing efforts did get him a parole and she saw him on a plane and off to California.

Now, in the gray hours of the early morning, she was at this new jail on a different errand. Sierra . . . what could have happened?

The jail yard was landscaped, the waiting room was spacious, with a great expanse of plate glass looking out on Atlanta's skyline in the misty distance. The black woman at the desk was courteous when Kate identified herself and said she had come in answer to a call from a young neighbor girl.

"You'll have to see the Major," the woman said, picking up a phone. To Kate's surprise, he was on duty, despite the hour. A young man in military khaki came out of a neighboring office, introduced himself as Major Riley, the warden, shook her hand, and led her down a corridor to a vast cell block. A female guard greeted them at the door and unlocked it, admitting them to a corridor lined with cells. Their occupants were in an uproar.

Sierra sat on the corridor floor, tears streaming down her face.

"What have they got her for?" Kate asked, turning to the Major.

"Prostitution," said the guard.

"Oh, no, not Sierra," Kate said. "She's only sixteen!"

The guard turned to one of the prisoners in a cell. "She come in with you, didn't she, Maybelle? What did she tell the officers her age was?"

"Well, eighteen, I think," Maybelle said unwillingly. "But she ain't no prostitute. She thought she would give it a try last night, but before she could turn a trick, the law got us both."

"Major, she's just a child," Kate said. "I know her family. They live up the road from me in the country. Let me take her home. I'll bring her back to court, if necessary."

The guard chortled. "It ain't prostitution now," she said triumphantly, looking at the Major with some satisfaction, for she knew something he apparently had not been apprised of in his front office.

"You didn't hear the alarm? Sir?" she added belatedly.

"I guess I was at breakfast," Riley admitted, abashed. "What happened?"

"She pushed Lorene against the bars of their cell. Knocked her out! Lots of blood. She's in the infirmary now."

"You know why she did," Maybelle said. "That big old dyke was trying to rape her!"

"I didn't see nothing like that," said the guard.

"How do you know?" Kate asked Maybelle. "Did anybody else see it?"

"Everybody *heard* 'em," said Maybelle. "But the queers—they ain't gon' testify against Lorene. This little white child ain't got a chance."

"Like hell," Kate said angrily. "Come on, Sierra," she said to the weeping girl. "Get on your feet. Major, can I take her somewhere so I can talk to her?"

"My office." The warden nodded to the guard to open the door. Kate put an arm around Sierra, and

they followed Major Riley to the front of the building.

The Major ushered Kate and Sierra into a small room that overlooked the front lawn. He offered them coffee and poured two cups, then he went outside, leaving them alone. Kate sat on a small plaid love seat and pulled Sierra down beside her.

"Start at the beginning," she said. "Do your parents know where you are? Or your aunt? Or your sister, Siesta?"

Sierra shook her head miserably. "After Charlie didn't rape me, they thought I couldn't get nobody. I thought I'd show 'em. I seen on television them prostitutes working them streets back of the old Biltmore Hotel. I thought I could do that—and make money besides."

Only then did Kate notice the girl wore false eyelashes and blue eye shadow and had dyed her blond hair. Her dress, slinky black polyester, with the skirt slit halfway up her thighs, was torn and bedraggled.

"You really fixed yourself up for the business, didn't you?" Kate commented dryly. "So then what happened?"

"Well, I met Maybelle, and we was gon' stick together. But that was a mistake. She's been out there a lot and the police knowed her and thought I was with her and they caught us both."

"And after that you got locked up?"

"They put me in a cell with this big hateful woman named Lorene, who right away grabbed me and tried to git on top of me on that bunk bed. She was pulling at my clothes and slobbering and kissing me. And all the others heard and were yelling and cheering."

Kate felt sick to her stomach and pushed away the cup of coffee the Major had set on the table at her elbow. This girl needs some real guidance, she thought.

"Did she attempt sodomy?"

"What's that?"

"Did she put her mouth on your privates or try to make you put yours on hers?"

"Yes'm," the girl whispered, ducking her head.

"Did you?"

"No'm, I did not. She tore my clothes and held me down—she sure was strong!—but I was so mad I pushed her offa me and suddenly I was stronger than her and I knocked her against the bars, over and over, until she fell down, and her head was all bloody."

"Oh my God," moaned Kate, putting her face in her hands. Then, taking her hands away, she looked at the frightened, smeary face of the teenager.

"I think you are a stone cold fool in the morning," she said, "but under the circumstances, you did the best you could."

"Well, can I go home now?"

"I don't think it's going to be that easy." Kate went to the door and spoke to the warden, who was sitting at his receptionist's desk, reading the morning paper.

"Major," she said, "I think this child was about to be sodomized and she acted in self-defense. I'd appreciate it if you'd let me take her home."

"Oh, I couldn't do that," the young prison officer said, getting to his feet. "She'll have to go before a judge. We have one here, and she could do that after nine o'clock. That's the best I can do."

"Well, can I use your phone to call a lawyer?"

"Yes, ma'am, you certainly can." He pushed the phone on the desk to her. "Do you need a directory?"

Kate shook her head. As much business as she had given Phil Brown in the last few days, his telephone numbers were fixed in her mind. She of course woke him up, and he mumbled sleepily, begging her to call him later at the office.

"Phil, this is urgent," she said. "A sixteen-year-old child has been mauled around in a rape-sodomy attempt, and I can't get her out of this jail.

"Hearing? I *know* she's entitled to a hearing, but that could take days—even weeks. I simply will not leave a little girl in jail with a bunch of rapists! You've got to get her out *now!*"

Phil mumbled something about bail and Kate screeched, "Sure I could sign a bail bond for her, but that'll take time. I need you *now*, Phil!"

Phil said he'd have to speak to the warden, and Kate handed the phone to Major Riley. She walked back to his office and saw Sierra, collapsed on the plaid love seat, which she was spotting with her tears.

Riley called from the outer office. "Phone for you, Mrs. Mulcay. Mr. Brown."

Kate picked up the receiver on the Major's desk and heard a gigantic yawn from Phil Brown. "Don't give me that, Phil," she said. "I'm sleepy too."

The attorney recovered quickly. "I'm not sure what I can do, Kate, but I'm on my way. Meanwhile, line up what witnesses you can—anybody who knows of the attempt on your little friend. The Major's going to let you talk to them—sort of put them on record, so we'll have them if we need them."

Kate hung up, looking at Major Riley in astonishment. Could he do that? It didn't seem legitimate to her.

"I don't think I'm within my authority to do this, but in view of the girl's age and Lorene's long history of abusing prisoners, I'm gon' let you gather what witnesses you can." He grinned. "Could lose my job over this, you know."

"Oh, no," said Kate, lying roundly. "I've done this loads of times. You are gon' let me take Sierra home, aren't you?"

"You can sign her bond," the Major said. "I've been told you have valuable property in north Fulton County."

"Thank you," said Kate. "Now, while I talk to witnesses, Sierra, you can go wash your face and comb your hair. Won't that be all right, Major?"

He nodded. "I'll send somebody with her."

Riley walked Kate back to the cell block and turned her over to the guard. "This is Mrs. Mulcay," he said. "Writes for the paper. Let her talk to anybody she wants to."

Kate walked along the cells, looking over the prisoners, and she shivered. They were a mean-looking lot, she thought, who had witnessed with interest Lorene's attempt to rape Sierra. Lorene was one of them, and were they free, they might well retaliate by punishing the girl with some form of violence.

For a start, Kate paused to talk to a very old black woman who sat on a vinyl sofa outside the cells. Kate introduced herself, and the old woman patted her on the arm with an emaciated hand. She did not wear a prison uniform but was dressed in a dark cotton dress with a white collar, a little pin at the neckline. She was a picture of old-fashioned respectability.

Kate looked at the guard inquiringly. Why was this prisoner different?

"Aunt Lucy is waiting to be transferred to Milledgeville," said the guard. "She ain't done nothing except get old and helpless. We keep 'em a day or two, till there's a load for the state hospital."

"Mistis," said the old woman, as if she had not heard the guard. "Will you tell my peoples I'm here and ax 'em to come and get me?"

"Yes, I will," Kate said. "Tell me their names."

The old woman raised her gray head proudly and recited a list of prominent Atlantans of another day, all of them dead now. "Nussed their chillun," she said softly. "They come and get me."

Kate had gone to the funeral of one of those Aunt Lucy had named, a philanthropist. And she remembered that another couple the old woman mentioned had died in the crash that killed more than a hundred Atlanta art lovers on takeoff from Orly airfield, near Paris. Perhaps the "chillun" would help.

"I'll find somebody, Aunt Lucy," she said. "Now, can you tell me what happened this morning to Lorene?"

"Mistis, she was atter that child. 'Twas God's hand that pushed her. God don't love ugly."

She'd be a good witness for Sierra if one was needed, Kate thought. A black gentlewoman, the kind everybody in the South loved. She hugged the old woman and turned toward the cells. "I'll find somebody for you," she called over her shoulder.

In the time when she was in the Major's office, calm had descended over the cell block. Prisoners were sprawled on their bunks as Kate proceeded from cell to cell. The common answer was "No'm, I didn't see nothing."

She was standing helplessly before a big silent woman who occupied the cell next to Lorene's. The prisoner turned her face to the wall and made no answer to Kate's questions until Maybelle, the prostitute who had been with Sierra, spoke up.

"Be ashamed of yourself, Laverne," she called. "You know what Lorene did to the younger prisoners. She got you started, didn't she? Well, this woman might write a nice piece about you for the paper if you'll cooperate."

"I don't know about that," Kate objected wearily. "I just want the truth."

"That's right," said Maybelle. "She don't want to see no little girl go to prison for defending her honor."

It sounded good to Kate, and it must have sounded fine to Laverne. She rose up on her bunk and said, "Lorene was always after the young'uns. That little girl this morning was lucky she could defend herself."

The guard, who now seemed eager to assist Kate, opened the door of the cell and let Laverne out, directing the two of them to the dayroom.

Celestine
Sibley

Laverne preceded Kate, as stately as a queen arriving at a ball. She sat on a vinyl sofa and patted the cushion beside her, in invitation to Kate. Her dark face was scarred with ancient knife cuts, and one eye seemed permanently closed, but Kate perceived the underlying beauty.

"Now what can I do for you?" Laverne asked, a hostess bestowing a favor.

"A lawyer for Sierra is coming very soon," Kate said, "and I want you to tell exactly what happened. I think we can take the child home where she belongs if we have a good strong witness to the fact that she did not attack Lorene but pushed her in self-defense."

"Shit, that's easy," said the woman. "She's nothing but a chile, and Lorene is a big ox and real mean."

There was a stir in the corridor, and Major Riley arrived with Phil Brown, still rumpled and sleepy, but conscientiously there.

Kate went to meet them.

"I've got two good witnesses," she said, grabbing Phil's arm. "Sierra was totally justified in what she did."

"Let me talk to them," the lawyer said. He looked at the Major for permission, and Riley nodded.

Laverne and Aunt Lucy were taken aside, and except for Aunt Lucy's occasionally becoming sidetracked about "my peoples," the two women agreed about Sierra's action as self-defense.

Major Riley said, "I'm gon' let you take the girl home. I may be wrong, and I may get in trouble for it, but—"

"Oh, I'm sure you won't," said Kate warmly. "You're doing the right thing. If there's any problem, I can always bring her back." If she doesn't get into something else stupid, Kate added to herself.

Sierra was brought out. She had cleaned her face of makeup but still, of course, wore the slinky, bedraggled dress slit up the sides. Her intention to wow the men who frequented old Cypress Street had failed, and the black dress simply made her look young and tawdry.

"I see you've still got on your church dress," Kate joked.

Sierra looked defiant. "I ain't got a church dress. I don't go to church."

"Wouldn't hurt," Kate said briefly, leading the way to the jailhouse entrance.

She thanked Phil Brown for coming. He smiled dubiously. "I didn't do anything. You did it all, as usual. If the warden gets fired, it's your fault."

"Oh, Phil, don't be a pessimist. You were the heavy artillery. You backed me up."

Phil looked ready to believe her. "By the way," he said as he walked her and Sierra to Kate's car. "The man who may buy your pianos would like to see them before the new year. Maybe the day after Christmas."

"Fine," said Kate, but she didn't feel fine about it. She hated to evict Shag and Warty.

Sierra got out at the Gandys', and Kate hurried home to get ready for work.

Jonathon was sitting in his truck in her driveway. He looked at his watch as Kate got out of her car.

Celestine
Sibley

She glared at him.

"I don't want to carp," he said cheerfully. "But you seem to've been gone all night. Case of the pot calling the kettle black?"

"I'm not calling you anything," Kate said sulkily, turning toward the back steps.

Jonathon was out of his truck and following her.

"Mind telling me where you were? It's none of my business, I know, but I care about you, Kate."

"If you must know," Kate said, "I was in jail." She wouldn't have told him, but the fact that he was in his truck instead of in Toddy's father's gift car was unreasonably mollifying.

Jonathon looked startled and then unbelieving.

"You, Kate? Not you. You were rescuing some hapless neighbor, huh?"

Kate nodded and pushed the kitchen door open.

"Sierra," she said. "Soliciting prostitution and defense against sodomy."

It sounded shocking, and the minister was shocked. "Oh, God," he whispered. "What a thing for you to be mixed up in! Kate, you can't make yourself responsible for all these troubled people."

"Please go," said Kate. "I'm very tired, and I have to get in to work."

He didn't move. "I've seen you lift spiders out of the sink instead of squashing them," he said, reaching out a hand to her. "I notice that you feed the squirrels just as you do the birds. Nobody else does that. They build barriers."

Kate brushed by the extended hand and headed for the stairs. "They get hungry too," she said over her shoulder. At the top of the stairs, she called back, "I also consort with roaches and ticks, but *not*"—her voice was strong—"with snakes and rats."

When she came out of the shower, with a towel wrapped around her, Jonathon was standing there with a fresh-made cup of coffee in his hand. "Here, drink this," he said. "It might sweeten your disposition."

Kate was torn. Jonathon was a good man, but he could be judgmental—as if he were in a position to judge others! She looked at the bed that she had vacated hours before. In her weariness, it was tempting; even more tempting was the big masculine presence. Would it hurt if he took her in his arms and to that bed? Warmth and strength—ah, she needed them.

Oh, Benjy, she thought, tell me what to do. Fitzgerald had written that when people died, they didn't tell you the road to take; you had to find it for yourself.

She took the coffee from Jonathon's hand and pointed to the stairs. "Go," she said. "I must get dressed. Unlike your little friend, I can't run around naked."

"You are being shrewish," he replied. "I'll go."

Kate wrapped herself in her robe and stood by the window to watch him back out of the driveway.

Suddenly she realized it was not a workday but Saturday, the day before church day. She looked forward to tomorrow, when she could go—not to his church but to her own, the austere white clapboard Presbyterian church where she and Benjy had worshiped. Sitting in the hard old pews and listening to the old hymns, she might get the comfort she had denied herself when she pushed Jonathon on his way.

Kate was ashamed at her age to have felt his presence and wanted him to hold her. That was for Toddy and her peers.

This day she would devote to herself. After attending to Snag and Warty's needs, she'd relax and read and try to forget about guilt and innocence for a day.

Arising Sunday morning, Kate looked over what her closet had to offer. No need of the new cream wool suit, without Jonathon to admire her. She pulled out a tired tweed suit and headed for the ironing board.

Later, dressed, she fed Pepper and Sugar and put out feed for the birds, noticing that a little gray squirrel waited on the wellhouse roof, switching his tail and eyeing the sunflower seeds.

She didn't mind feeding the squirrels too, as Jonathon had remarked. She rather liked watching them play on the rooftop and leap from tree to tree. And she did lift spiders out of the sink with a wooden spoon on a lot of mornings. When she and Benjy were new in the house, he had gently removed a snake from the kitchen and she had returned a frog to the out-of-doors. Were things like that a sign of weakness? Did she help her troubled "dirty-neck" neighbors to make herself feel good? She knew she didn't. She liked them and worried about them, and how would she explain to Miss Willie and the girls,

Sheena and Kim Sue, if she ever failed to respond to a call for help?

Even now she wondered if poor misguided Sierra was getting any comfort or encouragement from her family. What was the situation with her parents, anyway? Kate should probably go and talk to them—but what would Jonathon say to that?

Instead she brushed her hair and put on lipstick and went to church.

The little white clapboard building was filled, its second service of the morning. Kate smiled and spoke to friends who served as ushers, then she slipped into a back pew.

Hiram Scott, their longtime minister, who had retired ten years before, was back, serving as interim pastor while the search committee looked for somebody to replace young Dr. Harrison, who had gone on to a bigger, richer church in town. Dr. Scott preached the same seasonal sermon he had preached for many years, and Kate felt happy with it. Though the old man apparently wasn't going to heal her spiritual abrasions, the young tenor soloist sang a song that helped immeasurably: "Come, Ye Disconsolate." Kate followed it silently.

Come ye disconsolate, wher'er ye languish,
Come to the shrine of God, fervently kneel,
Here bring your wounded hearts, here tell your
    anguish.
Earth has no sorrow
That Heav'n cannot heal, that heaven cannot
    heal.

Heal Sierra, Kate prayed, and Shag and Warty and Beau and his family . . . and me.

The day was mild for late December, and a goodly crowd of worshipers lingered in front of the church to speak to the pastor, make dates to come to the candlelight Christmas Eve carol service, and exchange the news and gossip of the day. Two women approached Kate, and she recognized one of them as Miss Maria Beckman, whose garden was going to be on the Episcopal church benefit tour. She greeted Kate with a smile and a little hug.

"Child, I hear we're going to be on display at the same time—for the benefit of the Episcopalians!"

"I said I would," Kate admitted, "but I can't imagine anybody paying a cent to see my poor, pitiful yard."

"Don't you worry," said Miss Maria. "Mine is an eyesore at this season. But I have a new yardman, and he promises to spruce things up. Would you like to borrow him?"

"Yes, ma'am!" said Kate. "Anytime you can spare him. Send him over, or call me and I'll pick him up."

"Well, he's working for the Episcopal church part time, but I know you can persuade the rector—you know Dr. Craven?—to let you have him for a few days."

I may never see Dr. Craven again, Kate thought. But of course there was the garden in the spring; he would in all probability surface for that. She decided to go home and look over her patch and make plans for spring. The catalogs were coming in. It was a ritual she usually reserved for New Year's, but as the

Gandy sisters had pointed out, she was a lonesome, friendless woman. It was something to do.

The sky was a morose gray, and when she got home, a chill wind whipped around the corner of the cabin, tearing at the shingles on the roof. A skinny gray cat shivered by the back screen door.

"Who are you? Where did you come from?" Kate addressed the newcomer. Pepper and Sugar were indoors, fugitives from the weather. The cat shivered and cringed as if Kate had struck her. "You're pregnant, aren't you?" Kate observed, reaching out a hand to the visitor. A claw came out and raked her fingers.

"Oh, you mean thing!" Kate said, sucking her bleeding thumb. "You want food from me, you'd better mind your manners."

The cat growled low in her throat.

"Well, you've spirit, even if you haven't a decent body to hang it on." Kate looked at the scrawny frame supporting the swollen belly. "Wait here."

She pushed the cat aside and then opened the door to the kitchen. Milk and tuna fish, she decided, checking the cupboard. She tried to keep a can of fish for herself for those "lonesome" days when she was housebound with no real groceries in the kitchen and no enthusiasm for shopping or eating out. It was a reliable staple, but this was a starving cat. She would share.

Pepper and Sugar rose from their places—the hearth rug for Pepper and the back of the sofa for Sugar, who preferred a high perch when she could find them. Smelling the tuna, they followed Kate to the back porch.

"Wait here," she directed them. "I'll feed you in the kitchen. This is for Po' Nellie Gray." To make sure Pepper didn't lap up the milk and grab the canned fish with one swipe of his big tongue, Kate pushed the feeding bowls under a lawn chair where only something as emaciated as that cat could reach them.

Then she went indoors and filled bowls for the regulars. Once or twice she glanced out the window at the visitor, who ate with starvation's frenzy.

"I don't want you," she said, "but I'll feed you till I can find a home for you."

Out of sudden mischief, she thought of Jonathon. How would it be to tie a dirty ribbon around the cat's neck and present her to him? Would he turn out a starving cat?

Kate changed to wool slacks and a sweater and built up the flagging fireplace blaze. She stretched out on the sofa to the seed catalogs. Would there be time to get peonies in the ground and blooming for June? She had always wanted a pale-pink Eleanor Roosevelt she saw in the Wayside catalog. Far too expensive, but it would be stunning by the cabin door. She would order three. She had roses, but who ever had enough roses? She searched the old rose catalogs. There was one from a new nursery up the road by the old gold-mining town of Dahlonega, whose gold rush preceded that of the West in '49. Now it had roses—and such wonderful ones.

Kate read about Champneys' pink cluster, bred in South Carolina in the early nineteenth century and the ancestor of the charming Poinsette class. The picture showed a golden heart and a radial arrangement of pink petals. Kate really liked single roses best. That was the reason for her attachment to the old Cherokee, snowy petals and golden center, the state flower of Georgia. She had several and rejoiced when they bloomed.

This new nursery offered the Cherokee, with information that the owner was a rose "rustler," one of those people who stage "search and rescue" hunts for roses in old communities and on country back roads. She might just drive up to that nursery, but the catalog said it was closed for the Christmas holiday, and she compromised by making out an order for two more Cherokees.

She didn't know where she would plant them, and she was thinking about braving the blustery weather to tour her backyard, when a truck pulled into the yard and a deliveryman knocked at the door.

He was a handsome young deliveryman, and he obviously liked his job. "Red roses for a blue lady!" he said, handing Kate the slender florist's box.

"Oh my goodness," Kate mumbled. "Where are they from?"

"Card inside," said the boy. "Enjoy, enjoy!" and he was off down the steps.

They were indeed red roses, the stately American Beauty, which Kate liked least of all: a kind of commercial rose, it lasted only a day or two and usually cost the buyer lots of money. These particular roses were fresh and dewy and fragrant, though, and they moved her before her fumbling fingers could detach the card and read it.

"I'm the spider in your sink," said the note. "Love,
Jon."

Kate immersed the stems in a soup pot of water
while she looked for a vase, unable for a few minutes
to think about the sender. When she finished
arranging the roses in her grandmother's old blue
crockery pitcher, she sat a moment at the kitchen
table, just staring at them.

She should have savored them. How long had it
been since anybody, much less a handsome man,
had sent her roses? But all she could think was: Why?
Why do you do this, Jon? You know you don't love
me. Let it go. Get along with your life and your eager
little limpet.

She debated calling and thanking him. Surely he
had overreached in joking about the spider in the
sink. To call would be capitulation, and she wasn't
sure she even liked him anymore. She put on her
half-boots and heavy jacket and tied a scarf on her
head and headed outside for a walk.

Somehow when she walked in the woods she had
no taste for yard work. Indeed, the unplanted, the
untended, the natural, appealed to her more than
anything she could cultivate. The very weeds had
shape and symmetry that she could never achieve.
The brown fronds of dock remained upright, like
rusty iron standards, in winter. She usually gathered
a few for the brown-glaze pitcher she and Benjy had
bought at a roadside pottery years before. The little
green seed pods of Queen Anne's lace had risen
above rain and frost and were distributing on the
field and roadside the largesse of white blossoms to

come. Fields of broom sedge were golden in the winter light. Whenever someone singing "America the Beautiful" got to the part about "amber waves of grain," Kate, having practically no experience with waves of grain, visualized broom sedge. It was as beautiful as growing grain, she felt, even if it did not produce food or anything more useful than a hearth broom. Kate's country neighbors always had a bundle of the golden sedge bound around with string to make a broom, certainly one for the hearth, often one for porch and steps.

To encourage guests to depart, the sedge broom was placed in the corner with salt sprinkled around it. Kate had never tried this, but she was told it was a surefire expedient if you wanted to send somebody on his way. Should she have tried that on Jonathon?

She wished she could stop thinking about Jonathon. The memory of his eyes, his big hands on her shoulders, the dark timbre of his voice, were disturbing. She had taken a walk in the windy weather, which now had a promise of snow, to shake him out of her mind, but he kept coming back. That was all physical, she reminded herself, but what really concerned her was character, maybe heart and soul. Spiders in the sink was one thing, but he condescended to certain people, which to Kate was all the worse in a man of God, who should believe that everyone was a child of God, valuable in His sight, the unfortunate, worthy of the help of those more fortunate.

The woods path branched off along Shine Creek and turned with it. It would lead her eventually to

Miss Willie's house, and she found she had an urge to see the old woman. Since her absorption in the problems of Beau and Shag and Warty and Sierra, Kate seemed to have had no time for visiting the wise and comforting neighbor. As she approached the house, Pepper came out to greet her. She had wondered why the dog hadn't followed her on her walk. He had business at Miss Willie's, where there was always a plate of warm food for him and a spot on the hearth rug in front of the fire. He had apparently heard her approach up the rocky little path and asked to get out.

Miss Willie stood in the open door to greet her. "Lordamercy, child, come in out of the cold!"

A sifting of snow was visible on the porch, and Kate felt a flake slide off the collar of her jacket and down her neck. She ran the last few steps to the porch.

Miss Willie's warm old hands grabbed her, and an arm propelled her into the front room. "Take a chair," she said, "and I'll bring you a plate of chicken and dumplings. I was wondering why I cooked so much, but I reckon I was guided."

When Miss Willie said she was "guided," the implication was that a spiritual force had taken a hand in her life. Kate believed it—and wished for similar guidance herself.

She sat in one of the big rockers with its padding of many cushions, made by Miss Willie through the years. Easing off her boots, she extended her feet toward the slow-burning, rosy log in the fireplace. Even Miss Willie's fireplace fires seemed to burn at a deliberate, thoughtful pace, unlike Kate's, which often flashed and flared and burned out.

Bringing back a steaming bowl, Miss Willie walked softly and spoke softly.

"You got company?" Kate asked.

The old woman nodded. "Sierra."

"Miss Willie!" cried Kate, trying to keep her voice down. "What on earth are *you* doing with her?"

"Eat and I'll tell you," the old woman said, handing the bowl, with its creamy, fragrant chicken and dumplings, to Kate, who suddenly realized she had been bypassing meals lately.

"I went and got her," Miss Willie said. "I heard the child was in trouble. Oh, her own people love her, all right, but you know, Kate, loving don't always mean understanding." She was silent a moment, looking into the fire. "And sometimes even understanding ain't good enough. It's forgiving and hepping a person sometimes needs."

Kate chewed a delicate, feather-light dumpling. "Miss Willie, you *are* talking about Sierra, aren't you?" She didn't add, "and not me," but she didn't have to.

"I reckon I'm talking about humans," Miss Willie said, smiling crookedly and pulling up another rocker to the hearth. "That young'un has done foolishness, I know, but poking fun at her and rowing with her about it ain't hepping none. I thought she needed to sleep in my feather bed and eat my chicken and dumplings and maybe go to church. She went with me this morning, and you know what the preacher preached on? 'The Lord is nigh unto all

Celestine
Sibley

them that call upon him.' That's from the Book of
Psalms, he said, and there was another one, kind of
extry: 'Draw nigh to God and he will draw nigh to
you: cleanse your hands, ye sinners, and purify your
hearts, ye double-minded.'"

Kate sighed. "Oh, Miss Willie, you're talking to
me. I'm so double-minded I can't stand it."

"That preacher feller, ain't it?"

"Yes, ma'am."

"You think you love him, but you ain't certain
sure?"

"No, ma'am."

"Let it rest, Kate. Let some time pass. Ain't no
hurry, is there?"

Kate leaned over and held her hands to the fire. "I
don't know. He hinted that he wants to marry me,
but there's this pretty little girl who's after him, and I
think he likes that too. Marrying me might solve
some of his problems and some of mine, but . . . I
don't know."

"Wait, Kate," Miss Willie said decisively. "Don't be
hardhearted and hateful to him, but wait . . . wait."

How intuitive the old woman was! Hardhearted
and hateful Kate had been. She felt crowded in a corner, and she used everything against Jonathan.

She smiled at Miss Willie. "Okay, so you've taken
care of my problem. What are you going to do for
Sierra?"

Miss Willie smiled mischievously. "I'm a-using
you," she said. "I told her education is how you get to
be somebody—and you are the proof. You got a
good job you like. You are somebody, even in a big

place like Atlanta. You know governors and mayors and people like that. You can go where you like and do what you please, and you don't have to hang around a street corner at night to git a man to pay attention to you. They come to you." She paused and grinned. "Like the preacher feller."

"Aw, Miss Willie, you could find a better example than me."

"Naw, not in reach," the old woman said realistically.

"Well, you make a good case for it," Kate admitted, "but if you get the horse to water, how you gon' make her drink?"

"I'm a-going with her to that high school tomorrow, and I'm a-going to talk to the headman about gitting this child to learning. Ain't nobody's took a interest before. If she stays here with me awhile, she is gon' study them books."

If she doesn't have to go to jail, Kate said silently.

She thought of Beau, in jail already, and wondered if he was regretting his quixotic effort to take his father's place in the federal pen. Then there was the nagging feeling that Beau had not committed the crime. But who had, then?

She thought of Shag and Warty and their Christmas invitation. She had an impulse to invite Miss Willie. The old lady never went to Atlanta—not since the day when she walked thirty miles to the mule market, to get herself a beast for plowing. It might be fun to take her downtown and witness her reaction to Shag and Warty and their squatters' home in the fine old neighborhood that now was a slum.

"Miss Willie," she asked tentatively, "do you know what street people are?"

"Them people that pour concrete, I reckon. Or them policemen that blow whistles and wave your mule and wagon on."

Kate laughed. "I don't think Atlanta policemen would know a mule if they saw it. I doubt if there's been one on a downtown street since the funeral of Dr. Martin Luther King, Jr., when they hauled his coffin across town in a wagon."

"Bless the Lord," murmured Miss Willie. "Then what air street people?"

Suddenly Kate didn't want to humiliate Shag and Warty. After all, she was going to present them as hosts of a Christmas party.

"People with no place to live, who sit out on the sidewalk and collect money from passersby, are called street people."

Miss Willie was impressed. "People just give them money, without no obligation?"

The obligation of charity or guilt, Kate thought. She nodded.

"Ain't that a-begging?" asked Miss Willie.

The old woman would not approve of that, Kate knew. When a woman from one of the Roswell churches tried to persuade Miss Willie to accept a basket of groceries, she had run her off the porch with the broom. Nobody in her family had ever been beholden, and she didn't plan to start.

Kate fumbled for an explanation: Shag was a war veteran and Warty was disabled, and they were try-ing to make do in a vacant old house on the south side of town. Alone and friendless, they wanted to have a little Christmas celebration. They had asked Kate, and she would be happy to have Miss Willie ride into town with her on Christmas night.

"I'll take a jelly cake!" Miss Willie volunteered enthusiastically. "Menfolks always like a good jelly cake."

"Me too," said Kate, putting on her boots and preparing to leave. "Christmas night. Then it's settled."

Miss Willie followed her to the door. "Ease your mind, Kate," she said. "You'uns will work out the knots. Your preacher feller is like dodder, ain't he?"

"What do you mean?" Kate said, and she blushed.

"Oh, I seen you throw a piece of the dodder vine on a bush by the creek a few days ago."

It was the most childish thing Kate had done in years. When she first met Jonathon and became interested in him, she had pulled a piece of the little gold vine—variously called dodder and love vine—off a bush beside the road and thrown it on an alder bush down by the creek. It was a parasite, she knew, and she meant the creekside alder no harm, but the childhood ritual appealed to her. Swing the vine over your head three times, kiss it, and name your fellow. Throw it on a bush, and if it grows, he loves you.

She waited for Miss Willie to close the door and go back to the fire before she took the creek path.

Already, the host bush was trussed up in the fine golden vine. Neither sleet nor snow nor dark of night had stayed its determination to swamp—and maybe kill?—the alder. Kate stood on the rocky path and put out a hand for the tendril of gold.

Her gardener's instinct made her want to pull the dodder off to save the bush. But her woman's instinct made her latch onto the superstition. If dodder grows, he loves you.

Tucking the length of gold she had picked up into her jacket pocket, Kate headed back to her cabin. The weather had warmed up, the snow had stopped, and the sun was shining.

When she reached the yard, the kitchen phone was ringing.

"I didn't see you in church this morning," Jonathon said.

"I was there," Kate said defensively. "At the real church."

He laughed. "I told you I was going to preach on forgiveness. I took my text from Micah. 'He retaineth not his anger forever, because he delighteth in mercy.' I wish you the same."

"I delighteth in red roses," Kate said. "Thank you, Spider."

"Pleasure is mine," Jonathon said. "Young people's meeting this afternoon and supper for the communicants' class tonight. You want to come? You know, you could learn the catechism and be an inducted Episcopalian when you marry me."

"Marry you?" Kate exclaimed. "I hardly need an Episcopalian marriage to teach me the catechism. I learned it when I was a child."

"Did you learn that when a man wants to love and adore you for the rest of your life, you might say, 'Thank you very much'?"

Kate giggled. What was the idea, talking about marriage like two schoolchildren?

Jonathon persisted. "You need the minister to teach you. How about a lesson in God's out-of-doors tomorrow? The weatherman predicts fair and warmer. I have the loan of a canoe from my landlord. We could take a picnic supper and paddle down the river."

It sounded so wonderful that Kate couldn't remember why she had been angry. "I'll bring the food," she said. "What time?"

"Let's try for the sunset hour. I know a place where we can spread a blanket and enjoy the last light on the river. And I can instruct you," he added, an exaggerated leer in his voice.

The weatherman was right. The day was one of those that came as a lovely surprise even to the natives. Just when Georgians settle down for severe Christmas weather, the sun can pour warmth and light like melted butter over the earth. The wind turns benign, frost disappears, and people who have planned to have a snug Christmas indoors walk out in the sunshine to visit, to finish last-minute shopping, to exult in warmth. Everybody knows it is as treacherous as a Gulf Coast tropical disturbance, which can reach hurricane proportions at any minute. By the end of the day, the wind can rise, the rain can fall, and the temperature can cascade toward freezing. But for however long it may last, nobody complains.

Celestine
Sibley

Kate finished work at the office in record time and went by the market, not to stock supplies for Shag and Warty this time, but for a picnic supper for Jonathon and herself. Sandwiches would be easy to handle, but she had a fine picnic basket with little plastic boxes to hold salads and dessert and a Thermos for coffee. She had washed and ironed a picnic tablecloth bought at a yard sale years before and saved for a special occasion—which this boded to be, she thought happily, as she changed to blue jeans and a sweatshirt. Taking a bottle of wine from the refrigerator, she checked the cupboard for glasses—something nice, she decided, but not her best. Years ago, Benjy had started her on a Waterford collection, and she thought the sparkle of the little wineglasses would lend elegance to the picnic by the river; but traveling in a canoe was precarious always, and if she had to swim or wade ashore, she would hate for those sparkling glasses to be picnic casualties.

Sheena and Kim Sue arrived as she was putting the picnic basket in her car.

"Where you goin', Miss Kate?" asked Sheena.

"Kin we go with you?" asked Kim Sue.

"Not this time," Kate said, hating to look at the disappointment on the two freckled faces. "This is a grown-up outing. I have been invited, so it wouldn't be polite for me to bring other people."

"We ain't other people," Kim Sue said. "We could be a hep to you. We'll take pitchers with our Kodak."

"I know," said Kate. "You always are a help. But this time Mr. Craven is taking me on the river in a canoe, and there isn't room in a canoe for more than two people."

"We-ell," said Sheena, admitting defeat.

The Gandy girls walked down the road, looking dispirited and abandoned. She hardly ever turned them down when they wanted to accompany her on some junket, Kate thought, but this outing with Jonathon was more than a ride in a two-person canoe. He had suggested much more, and to her surprise, she wanted to hear about love and marriage—on a blanket on a riverbank at sunset.

I'm getting old and sappy, Kate told herself. My life is all right without a man in it. Why do I yearn after this man, when I'm not really sure of him?

Before she had found a satisfactory answer, she arrived at the little boat dock in front of Jonathon's rented house on the Chattahoochee. A red canoe was tied to the dock, and Jonathon was busying himself about it. A plaid blanket was folded neatly in the stern.

Just as Kate parked her car, the Gandys' badly dented new BMW drew up beside her. Kim Sue and Sheena leapt out, and Mrs. Gandy rolled down the window and smiled at Kate.

"Girls told me you all were gon' take a little ride on the river," she said.

Just then, a small motorboat, which had been playing around with the strong river current, pulled into the dock, and out stepped Toddy, smiling angelically at Jonathon as she tied up next to the canoe. Jonathon seemingly ignored her—and Hettie, who remained in the boat—and climbed the bank toward Kate and Mrs. Gandy.

"I'm sorry I can't take the girls," he said. "As you can see, the canoe is a two-person craft. I'm taking Kate."

Toddy had followed him up the bank, looking sumptuous in a blue blazer and white shorts, with an expanse of perfect young sun-browned legs below.

"The girls can ride with Hettie and me," she said. "Our boat is big enough, and I'll look after them."

"Well, thank you," said Mrs. Gandy, always relieved to get rid of her daughters. She lost no time in starting up the BMW and taking off.

"Great!" cried Kim Sue and Sheena together. "Will you let us steer?"

"Might," said Toddy amiably. "Come on."

They climbed into the little runabout, squealing and stepping high to avoid the water in the bottom. Jonathon stood watching them a moment. Toddy took her seat next to Hettie in the stern, pressed the starter, and whirled the little craft out toward midstream.

Jonathon gave Kate a pained smile. "Alone at last," he murmured. But he was wrong. Toddy slowed her engine and waited until Jonathon had untied the canoe and pushed off from the bank. From his seat in the stern, he faced Kate, who was seated in the bow, and began paddling easily toward the middle of the river.

Toddy revved up her engine and circled them, rocking the little canoe and splashing Jonathon and Kate with its wake.

"Go on!" Jonathon yelled. "Go on! You're going to swamp us!"

Toddy gave a mock salute and headed back for midstream. The Gandy sisters, white-faced and anxious from the unaccustomed experience of boating on the river, were silent.

"Jonathon, let's go back," Kate said. "That reckless child might drown us all.

"Ah, no," said Jonathon, although he seemed to hesitate. "She's just a kid showing off. She's gone now."

They heard the motorboat somewhere beyond the bend in the river, and Kate relaxed. She had been on the Chattahoochee but had forgotten how beautiful it was. It originated as a brook in the mountains and grew wider and deeper as it approached the Gulf of Mexico. Until recent years, riverboats had traveled up it as far as Columbus. There was a Confederate gunboat in a museum there to commemorate its days as the port of West Georgia.

The city of Atlanta drew its water from the Chattahoochee. Kate was never sure how it could be sufficiently purified, but she thought it tasted good. All Georgia children learned Sidney Lanier's "Song of the Chattahoochee," and now, as she listened to the splash of Jonathon's paddle and the murmur of the river over and around rocks near the shoreline, she wished she could remember the poem. Only the opening lines came to her:

> Out of the hills of Habersham,
> Down through the valley of Hall,
> I hurry amain
> To reach the plain . . .

And after that she was stuck. She couldn't think poetry anyhow. The little motorboat was back, racing toward them, cutting away, darting back and circling, its engine roaring, Toddy waving, Hettie laughing, and the Gandys clutching each other fearfully.

"Go on, Toddy!" Jonathon cried again, waving his paddle. "You'll swamp us!"

"Good for me!" yelled the girl.

"Toddy, you're getting too close!" yelled Hettie.

Toddy steered away from the canoe and back toward midstream, and in a few minutes her boat was once again out of sight around the bend.

"I'm sorry," Jonathon said, looking at Kate's anxious face.

"Look, I can swim," she said, "but I'm not sure about the Gandys. The way that girl is carrying on . . ."

"We're out to have fun," Jonathon said. "Let's not spoil it."

The spoiling, Kate thought, was being done by that gorgeous child in the motorboat, but she said no more. If Toddy came close again, she was going to call to her to put life jackets on Sheena and Kim Sue. But she had apparently decided to go on down the river.

When Kate had seen their feckless mother abandoning the girls on the riverbank, she should have called off her picnic with Jonathon and taken them back home. Sheena and Kim Sue were still just girls and good ones, and she didn't want them, even on dry land, exposed to the irresponsible behavior of Jonathon's limpet sexpot.

Kate's glance wandered along the shore. The river itself was seductive. Because it was December, there were no other boats out. Apparently, people didn't trust the wonderful windfall summer weather. The lush green of the willows and laurels along the banks gave an illusion of summertime, and the water itself was deep-green velvet. A few new, handsome, many-windowed houses had been added to the handful of weathered homesteads, such as Jonathon's doctor landlord's, on the steep bank overlooking the river. But there were still wild spaces where old river fishermen gathered to tie up their vessels and build fires to cook their catches.

The Chattahoochee Nature Center—where Kate had taken Kim Sue and Sheena once to visit a redtailed hawk that had been rescued, wounded, from the roadside—had grown in size and facilities. It had its own boat dock and an enticing picnic area with playground equipment nearby. She should bring the girls back someday.

Jonathon's eyes were on Kate's face. "You don't look happy," he said, "like a girl who is getting engaged. That's what this outing is about, you know. You're supposed to see you can have fun even with a preacher. You're supposed to find you want to keep me."

Kate smiled weakly. "Don't be silly," she replied. "I'm not a girl, and my life has all the 'fun' that I can stand. Besides, you come with an unacceptable attachment."

A serious look crossed Jonathon's face. "I've been meaning to talk to you about that, Kate. You see, as a

preacher, I must keep certain things in confidence, but I also can't allow them to ruin my personal life."

"Whatever are you talking about?" Kate asked.

"Toddy. She came to me as a preacher, and I couldn't turn her away."

She wanted more than that, Kate thought. "Did you take advantage of that young girl?"

Before he could answer, their eyes were drawn by a shout from a big rock across the river. It was the grandfather rock of the Chattahoochee, used by kids in the summertime as a spot to dive from. Now it was occupied by Toddy, stark naked. Standing next to her was Hettie, fully clothed. They appeared to be arguing.

Toddy's young body was beautiful, almost luminous in the fading light. Suddenly Kate saw that above the magnificent thighs, the rounded stomach and shapely young breasts had an unexpected heaviness. The child is pregnant! Kate thought.

Toddy had her arms stretched out, pointing at their canoe, while she yelled something at Hettie. Just then Hettie burst into tears and ran down toward the boat. Toddy scrambled behind her and teetered on the rocks.

"Be careful or you'll slip!" Jonathon cried.

Sheena and Kim Sue were out of the motorboat and on the bank, getting ready to climb up the slippery side of the big rock.

"Girls, don't!" Kate cried. "You might fall. The water is cold. Stay there. We'll come get you!"

Then a shrill keening split the air, and Toddy's nude young body flailed off the rocks.

"I'll have to get her," cried Jonathon, kicking off his moccasins and pulling his sweater over his head. "That current is strong, and there's glass down there."

"Give me the paddle," Kate ordered, reaching for it. "I'll get the Gandys. They might fall in too."

Did Toddy's dark, curly head emerge for a second as Jonathon approached her with his strong, swift strokes through the fast-running river current? Kate thought she saw the girl, but she, too, was fighting the current, with paddle and canoe, and she wasn't sure.

Sheena and Kim Sue clung to a spindly willow tree and struggled to keep from slipping from the bank into the river.

"Hold on, girls," Kate ordered. "Hold on. You'll be all right. When I get the canoe close to the bank, don't jump in—the canoe will overturn. Ease yourselves in and lie down."

For a wonder, the Gandys obeyed, and because they were wet and the air was freshening, she threw them Jonathon's blanket, the one intended for their picnic. Only then did she turn to look for Jonathon and Toddy. Neither of them was visible.

Hettie sat in the motorboat, sobbing. "That mean-spirited tramp!" she cried.

Kate thought of asking the girl what she meant, but she was too busy moving the canoe away from the bank, to give Jonathon room to pull Toddy to shore when he got her. But he didn't get her. He came up, shaking water from his eyes and spitting it out of his mouth.

"I can't find her," he gasped. "She's not down there!"

Kate had been a strong swimmer in her youth. She knew she was out of practice now, but she kicked off her shoes and shucked her sweater.

"I'll help you look," she called, easing over the side. She pulled herself onto the bank by the Gandys' willow tree and hit the water from there.

"Kate, don't," she heard Jonathon say, as the cold water closed over her.

The bottom of the river was murky, and there *was* glass down there. Kate hated opening her eyes, but she was having no luck finding the girl with her hands, and she knew she could hold her breath only a little while.

She heard Jonathon dive down again, and she followed his long body toward the river's channel.

She swam to the shore with the idea of checking downstream and on the opposite bank, in case the girl had surfaced and swum or floated away.

The sun she and Jonathan had planned to see set had disappeared behind a bank of clouds close to the horizon, and Kate realized she was shivering when she pulled out of the water and the air struck her.

"Have you seen her anywhere?" she asked the sisters as she attained the bank.

"No, Miss Kate," whispered Sheena.

Jonathon had surfaced near the middle of the river and was swimming hard against the current.

"Start the boat," he called when he got closer. "We better go for help."

Kate reached for her sweater and her shoes and got in the motorboat with Hettie. Her experience at her beach cottage on the Gulf Coast made it easy for her to start this small river craft. She helped the sisters, still clutching the blanket, into the bow from the canoe and eased the throttle down to idle until Jonathon climbed out of the river, dripping and coughing up water he had swallowed.

They had passed a raft-rental place upstream, and Kate turned the boat and gave it the throttle. In a matter of minutes, they saw a few men around the rental dock. Jonathon cupped his hands around his mouth and yelled, "Help! A drowning! By the big rock! Come, follow us!"

Two of the men on the dock jumped into a launch that was tied there. Kate swung the little motorboat in a wide circle and headed back to the rock.

"Somebody call the police! Call an ambulance!" she yelled over her shoulder to the dock, and a young boy started at a dead gallop up the bank toward the rental office.

Hours later, Toddy's body had not been found. Divers had arrived and were combing the riverbottom. The girl's parents were there in a well-equipped pontoon boat they had borrowed from a friend. They took Kate and Hettie and the girls aboard and found Kate some dry clothing, belonging to the couple who owned the boat.

As darkness settled on the river, the fire department arrived with floodlights. Jonathon, still in his wet clothes, was busy showing the searchers where

Toddy had jumped and describing how he and Kate had tried to find her.

One of the divers grabbed the ladder on the side of the pontoon boat and spoke to the Dicksons.

"The current may have taken her downriver. We're gon' move to the 1-75 bridge."

"We'll go with you," said Toddy's father.

"I'd better take these girls home," Kate said. And call the newspaper office, she added to herself. As an afterthought, she thought of the shock that awaited Mrs. Dickson if they brought her daughter's body up stark naked in front of all the search party. And pregnant—did the mother know that?

She wondered if she'd better prepare the mother— for the nudity, at least. "Toddy will be cold," she began, nodding toward the chest from which she'd taken sweatpants and a sweater. Mrs. Dickson gave her a frigid thank you.

Kate couldn't help but wonder if a woman with such carefully coiffed hair, such flawless makeup— eye shadow, yet—could be as anxious as she purported to be. I don't know why I think a worried mother has to be frowsy and disheveled to be real, she thought in self-disparagement.

Transferring back into Toddy's motorboat, Kate, with Hettie and the Gandys as passengers, backed it into the river.

At the dock in front of Jonathon's cottage, she told Hettie to wait there, while she helped the girls, who huddled in Jonathon's now damp and muddy blanket, into the back seat of her car and started the engine and the heater.

"You'll be warm in a minute," she said.

"Miss Kate," Sheena called, "we heard them girls arguing about some wicked things before Toddy fell in."

"Yeah, they called each other tramps and said they gonna kill each other!" added Kim Sue.

"They both said they gonna go talk to Beau—that's who they arguing over."

Kate thought about this for a moment. "Stay put, girls, and I'll be back as fast as I can. I have to call my office."

Kate doubled back to the boat dock, where Hettie was sitting on the grass.

"What's this I hear about you and Toddy screaming you'd kill each other?" she asked as gently as she could. Kate saw there were tears on Hettie's cheeks.

"Toddy wanted everything I had, Miss Mulcay. Seems like everyone does."

Kate couldn't decipher whether this girl was angry or distraught. "This is about Beau, isn't it?" Kate asked.

"She was pregnant with his child! Beau and I were going to be married someday. I should have killed her myself!" she wailed.

If Toddy was pregnant with Beau's child, did that mean Jonathon had been telling the truth all along? But what about Toddy's nudity at his house? "Hettie, I'm going to call my office, and then I'm going to drive you home. Now take a deep breath and meet me at the car out front."

Kate tried the door to Jonathon's little house,

which was unlocked, as she supposed it would be. She went straight to the telephone on a table by the window. While she waited for the city desk to answer, she looked around the book-filled living room. Very tidy, as she expected of the minister. The small kitchen beyond was not quite so orderly. Plates were soaking in the sink—two plates, she noticed. Apparently, he'd had company for a meal.

Kate turned back to the living room as the city desk answered.

"Whatcha got for us now, Katie?" asked Mike King. "We already got one body being pulled out of the river. You got another?"

"No, I guess it's the same one," Kate said, sighing. "A young girl?"

"Yeah, lodged against a piling of the I-75 bridge. Buck nekked, they tell me."

"That's the one," Kate said. "You covered on it?"

"More covered than the corpse." Mike laughed at his own joke. "Got two people up there."

"Then you don't need me," Kate said, relieved. "If you do, call me. I'm going home. Got some children to deliver."

"The notorious Gandy sisters?" Mike asked. "If they were witnesses, we better talk to them." Kate had forgotten that most of her colleagues at the *Searchlight* knew Sheena and Kim Sue.

"Not this time," Kate said. "They were with me."

"Okay, Katie," Mike said. "Take off."

Kate hung up the phone and stood there a minute, looking at Jonathon's home base, his things. There was the faint smell she associated with him—

whiskey and tobacco and coffee. The top paper on the stack on the desk had, in his neat handwriting, what she took to be the beginning of a sermon: "Fight the good fight of faith, lay hold on eternal life, whereunto thou art also called. 1 Timothy 6:12."

Did Jonathon have to fight for his faith? she wondered, and pity for the man rose up in her heart. She felt sure now he was a good man—or at last so she thought.

The Gandy sisters were waiting for her in the car, their faces pressed against a window, watchful and expectant as hungry coons.

"Did you find out anything?" Sheena asked as Kate got in the front seat.

"What are you talking about? I just spoke to Hettie and used the phone."

"Aw, you know. Ev-i-dence," said Kim Sue, giving full weight to each syllable.

"Listen," Kate said, turning to face them. "I want you all to stop this stuff. Toddy slipped off the rocks, poor girl, and Hettie is having a very hard time with it. I want you to cut this out."

She started the car, then heard a whisper and turned again, to see Sheena's mouth close to Kim Sue's ear.

"What are you saying?" she demanded.

Sheena ducked her head, shamefaced and bashful.

"Nothin', Miss Kate."

Kate sighed and waited for Hettie, who was walking toward the car.

■ ■ ■

Kate left Hettie off at her house, then dropped the girls at their parents' trailer. They seemed so subdued that she was touched. She nearly laughed when they turned and, as she had taught them, said demurely, "Thank you for taking us, Miss Kate. We had a good time."

A good time . . . Oh Lordy, I hope I never have such a time again as long as I shall live. She was cold and bone tired, too tired to light the fire that was laid in the fireplace, only energetic enough to feed Pepper and Sugar and totter upstairs to the shower and to bed.

She thought Jonathon might call her and was relieved that he didn't. What would she say to him? Looks like you may have been telling the truth after all? No, best not to make things any more difficult than they already were. There would be a funeral, and Jonathon would have to handle it. The Dicksons were prominent members of Saint Margaret's. She wondered what Jonathon would say. Would he quote the psalm that said, "There is a river the streams whereof make glad the city of God"? No, it would be tactless for the Dicksons to hear any more about rivers.

Exhausted, Kate fell asleep immediately, too weary to cope with the problems that beset her.

Much later—the clock on the bedside table said 2:00 A.M.—she heard Pepper bark, but then he was silent. She thought she felt a breeze from the stairwell, and she wondered if the back door was open.

Now alert and half afraid, she sat up in bed. Her heart was pounding, her throat was dry and scratchy. "Who's there?" she managed to call.

There was no answer, but she thought she heard the brush of footfalls on the kitchen floor below, then the sound of the back door closing. Somebody had been in her house!

Fearfully, Kate put her feet on the floor and reached for her robe. Whoever it was might still be downstairs. She grabbed her flashlight and tiptoed to the stairwell. The draft of chilly air was still strong.

Scarcely daring to breathe, she eased down the steps. The living room was in darkness. She could barely see her own faithful rocking chairs, much less any lurking human being. She scoured the room with the beam from her flashlight, and finding nobody, she reached for the light switch and flooded the room with brightness.

"Hello, Kate," came a voice from behind her. She whirled and saw Jonathon standing in the kitchen.

"What on earth are you doing, snooping around my house in the middle of the night!" Kate almost shrieked. "You nearly scared me to death!"

"I came to say goodbye," he said somberly.

"Goodbye? Where are you going?"

"I don't know yet."

"What about your church? What about Toddy's funeral?"

He shook his head. "I have been dismissed. Somebody from another church will handle the funeral."

"Who dismissed you and why?" Kate cried.

"I think you know," Jonathan said, his gray eyes

gentle on her face. "Toddy was pregnant, Kate."

Suddenly she was incensed. "But I thought she was pregnant by Beau!"

A grim smile crossed Jonathan's face, the first one Kate had seen in days. "And now you think *I* was responsible?" He chuckled. "I was only responsible for counseling the girl—she came to me because she didn't have anywhere else to turn."

Kate thought this over. "Then why did Toddy spend so much time naked in your presence?"

"Toddy had delusions, Kate. She thought if I became interested in her, we could live happily ever after and she would avoid being scorned by her parents."

"Then what happened?" Kate asked. "How did everything end up this way?"

"I failed, Kate. I couldn't get her to listen, and I should have taken this to someone else—probably her parents. Or you. I'm sure you would have known what to do, but it spun out of control, and now a poor young soul has been lost."

"That was not your fault, Jonathon."

"It's not about fault. It's about my involvement, and I can't continue with the church here. I'm so sorry, Kate. I have to find another job, another church. I agreed to leave." His voice dwindled to silence. Then he squeezed Kate's hand and gave it back to her, as if he were presenting her with a gift. "I had no right, but I loved you. . . ."

Jonathon opened the door and walked out into the night.

Kate stood inside, watching till he was out of view.

■ ■ ■

The funeral, it turned out, was not to be at the church but at Atlanta's old and once stylish funeral home. There were many handsome and spacious funeral homes now, but Patterson's had got there first, with English antiques and landscaped grounds and even a rose garden. The feeling in Atlanta was that if you weren't buried from Patterson's, you were a newcomer or at worst nouveau riche. The Dicksons wouldn't have wanted anything like that. Besides, the downtown obsequies made it easier for Mr. Dickson's business friends to attend—and they were out in full force.

Kate, leaving the newspaper office a couple of miles away, had difficulty finding a seat in the chapel. A canon from Saint Philip's Cathedral, the Episcopal mother church, did the service, and Kate was touched by its simplicity. No eulogy, only one hymn from the chapel's speaker system, a psalm, and a prayer. Mrs. Dickson clung to her husband's arm and wept quietly on the front row, every hair in place.

Harriet Amelia Marylinn Caroline Amy Todd Dickson was at rest. Her friend Cece got to Kate at the side door, as she headed for the parking lot. Cece clutched at her hands and sobbed.

"Will Toddy go to heaven, Mrs. Mulcay?" the girl asked. "She was so fast, so bad!"

"I'm sure she will," Kate said, wondering.

"She hated you, Mrs. Mulcay. Mr. Craven told her he wanted to marry you, and she was so jealous she could have killed you."

"I'm sorry," Kate said. "I'm sorry. I've got to go."
She hurried to her car and backed out of the lot,
blinded by tears.

Jonathon had told the girl but had not been firm
with her. For Kate to have thought she was falling in
love with a man of such weakness, to have encour-
aged him at all, was a mistake.

She felt lonely and grim and un-Christmasy,
although office parties were starting up all over the
newspaper building when she arrived, and in the
company cafeteria a group from Circulation wore
Santa Claus caps and sang carols. She should check
on Shag and Warty, she knew, but she lacked the
energy for the trip down to Bass Street.

Then Philip Brown called her.

"First to wish you a Merry Christmas, Kate," he
said. "Two days to go, but I wanted to get my greeting in on time this year. Since my mother died, I
usually sleep through Christmas and neglect my
friends."

"Ah, Phil, that's not a bad way to spend the day,"
Kate assured him. "It leaves you all rested for the
new year. Christmas parties can be exhausting."

"That may be, but don't forget we are invited to
one on Bass Street. Christmas Eve, isn't it?"

Kate sighed. She had forgotten.

"Ah yes," she said, rallying. "I suppose they are
expecting us. I'll run down there after work and
make sure."

"May I pick you up on Christmas Eve?"

"I'd like that," Kate said, "but I'll be driving in from the country. My neighbor Miss Willie has promised to come with me."

"Then I'll escort two ladies," said Phil gallantly.

Kate stopped for milk and bread and eggs on the way to Bass Street, uncertain what, if anything, the two men had left but buying from habit as she bought for herself. She was not surprised to find that the kitchen was warm. They had discovered a backup coal pile in the garage. But she *was* surprised at how clean it seemed, swept and scrubbed. Foodstamp barked a welcome from the back door, and the two men relieved her of her shopping bags and trundled their one chair up to the stove for her.

"I came to see if you are still planning your Christmas Eve party," she said, poking her feet toward the oven door, which poured a nice warmth into the room.

"That we are," said Shag. "Engraved invitations have already gone out—to the governor, the mayor, and the police chief."

"He's full of shit, Miss Kate," said Warty. "We got some friends, but ain't none of them in high places, excepting you."

"Well, I'm coming with two others—Mr. Brown, a very nice lawyer, and Miss Willie Wilcox, an elderly friend and neighbor of mine. What kind of food shall I bring?"

The men looked at one another uncertainly. "You know, we got food stamps due at the welfare office," Shag finally said. "If you could pick them up and

take them to the store, we'd have a-plenty of rations for the party."

Kate shook her head. She could just imagine applying for food stamps and having clerks and social workers rally around, recognizing her from her picture in the paper.

"No," she said. "Leave them until you get out of here, which you're going to have to do any day now. Tell me what you want me to bring, and I'll shop for you before I go home tonight."

Shag looked at Warty's gaunt face, which was unnaturally red in the heat of the room. "What say?" he asked.

"Miss Kate," began Warty boldly. "I know you are a lady used to turkey and dressing at Christmas time. But what you say to bringing us the makings of a nice pot of stew? I'm pretty good at hobo stews. Lots of experience, you know." He laughed diffidently.

"Sure," Kate said agreeably. "You think a chuck roast and potatoes and carrots? What else?"

"Findings," Warty said. "Anything you got in your icebox you think might go bad. Celery, tomatoes— you got any parsnips? They add taste. Dried beans fills out a stew, makes it go a long way. If I was out of here and could check garbage cans and walk down by the railroad trestle, I expect I'd find plenty for the pot. Maybe a squirrel or a rabbit the train hit—they flavorsome."

"You stay indoors and out of sight," Kate said. "I can get the 'findings' for you."

"I know you can," Warty acknowledged. "I expect

you're a reliable cook. You ought to have a husband to feed."

I almost did, Kate thought bleakly. Jonathon, where are you now in that old rattletrap truck of yours? What will *you* do for Christmas? She thought of how handsome he looked in his black robe and the scarlet stole he would have donned for the Christmas season. She remembered lines from a psalm she could hear him reciting in his deep, resonant voice: "The Lord sets prisoners free; the Lord opens the eyes of the blind; the Lord lifts up those who are bowed down."

She was silent, listening to the clink of the stove.

The men watched her, until she sighed and stood up.

"Anything else?" she asked. "Bread, butter, maybe rice?"

"Ah, no," said Warty. "You done give us a peck of flour. I'll make a hoecake to dip in the gravy."

They walked her to the door.

"We didn't tell you, Miss Kate," Shag said, "but those friends we mentioned? We've asked a few of them to come. They ain't gon' be looking to stay, but they'd ruther celebrate Christmas here with us than in a shelter, and we made them welcome. It that all right?"

Kate paused with her hand on the cracked brown porcelain doorknob. Bringing these two into Miss Millicent's old house had been risky enough. She was fearful of expanding the crowd. "I don't know," she said uncertainly.

"Some of 'em is pretty good with music," Shag offered tentatively. "When we used to ride trains and

camp out under a trestle, we had some bodacious
singing."

What the hell, Kate thought. It's Christmas.

"Okay," she said. "Keep 'em in line. No fights, no
drunks, no setting the house on fire."

Shag was wounded. "They *friends*," he said with
dignity. "They ain't gon' do nothing to trouble you."

Warty giggled. "Don't be too sure," he said. "You
ain't 'sociated with Flippy Nell and Wingy Tolbert in
a while. They could get fractious."

Shag withered him with a glance. "They will be as
good as a Baptist preacher, Miss Kate. I promise you
that."

Kate wasn't sure what his promise was worth, but
she was too tired to debate the question—and she
still had to shop for the makings of hobo stew. She
didn't think until she was well on her way down
Georgia Avenue, past the old stadium, now being
razed, that after all she had told them, Shag and
Warty had had to leave the house to get word to their
friends about the party. Amazingly, they seemed not
to have gone out for liquor; being in residence in the
Clay mansion appeared to have sobered them up.
Well, in a day or two they would be back on the street
again and, also, back to their old ways. Too bad.

Warty's evident preference for rabbits and squirrels for his stew made her think of the old Municipal
Market on Edgewood. It had opened during the
Great Depression, as a place where Georgia farmers
could sell their produce and strapped Atlantans
could shop cheaply. She had been there many times
with that great cook her father, who liked things the

A & P didn't always carry, such as kidneys and tripe and brains. He bought fish there, and cracklings for his superb corn bread, and souse meat, derived from a hog's head. Later, as a reporter, she had gone there to do a story about the herbs and roots mountain farmers brought in and the kaolin, or white clay, that old people called "earth eaters" actually consumed.

The market had lost its hold on many Atlantans during the postwar years of affluence, and Kate had not been there in years. Now, if Warty needed a rabbit or a squirrel for his stew, it was the only place to get such a thing.

She turned off the South Expressway into Edgewood, a street that once was beautiful, with trees lining it on both sides, but now was a grubby boulevard of little shops, garages, and an occasional nonflourishing ethnic bar or restaurant. Old Grady Hospital and the new Grady, a concrete structure half a block away, overshadowed it. The market was busy tonight, but Kate had little trouble finding a parking space behind it. Many of its customers lived in walking distance of Capitol Homes, the huge public housing project, and some, of course, in the apartment buildings that had sprung up near the Martin Luther King, Jr., "birth house" and center, a few blocks away. Kate found a space between a truck and an old but gloriously waxed and burnished yellow Cadillac. A few men lounged around a portable cooker on the sidewalk, offering pork skins for sale. Kate paused, thinking they might be a greasy but tasty addition to Shag's party, but she didn't buy any.

The market had changed. Even its name was dif-

ferent; during the town's preparation for the Olympics, it had been changed to the Sweet Auburn Curb Market. It was neither. Sweet Auburn, the main black business street, was a block away. And it was not a curb market but a collection of stalls within a cavernous building as big as an airplane hangar.

Stalls were not as numerous as they had been in the past. There were FOR RENT signs on many, and Kate's mountain friends who grew their own turnips and collards and corn had been replaced by black, Chinese, and Hispanic entrepreneurs. The merchandise, though, was much the same.

Kate toured the market, looking at ox tails and pig tails and mounds of snowy "precleaned" chitterlings. She paused by thick bacon and smoked neck bones, enormous cow tongues and one case of cow feet.

"How do you cook those?" she asked the black man behind the counter, pointing to the big hoofs, which still bore pasture and stall stains.

"I chop 'em up for you, and you make a soup."

"Do they have meat on them?" she asked, thinking of Warty's stew.

"No, ma'am. Just bone and skin. You do better with pig feet."

Kate shook her head and moved on.

One stall offered bundles of little sticks, and, inquiring, she learned they were yellow root, with which to brew a tea for "the high blood" and arthritis. She bought a dollar's worth to add to Miss Willie's Christmas presents. Miss Willie was respectful of such remedies. Packages of kaolin were in the next stall, and Kate, who had never had the nerve to sample the white clay, picked up a package and was surprised to see it now had a legend, like a prescription at the drugstore: "Kaolin, white—cleanser, adhesive; pharmaceutical supply. Not suggested for human consumption." The FDA had taken a hand. She put it back and moved on past goat meat and pig ears to the seafood market, where for some reason rabbits were sold. They no longer hung in their skins from overhead hooks but were skinned and cut up and packed in ice in the showcase. A sign said WILD TRAPPED RABBITS $6.99. Pricey, Kate thought, comparable to a chuck roast and stew meat at Kroger's, but she bought one anyhow, asking the Chinese clerk to pack it with ice.

She would deliver it the next morning.

Back at the office, she found there was one message on her voice mail. She hoped it was from Jonathon, but she had a feeling it wasn't. If she had believed in him more, she might have climbed in his truck and gone with him wherever he decided to travel.

The message turned out to be from Beau Forrest. He sounded ebullient. "I'm doing okay," said the voice. "Wanted to wish you a merry one. They give us time at Christmas to talk to our loved ones, and I convinced them to let me call you. Do me one favor, please? If you see Hettie, tell her I'm doing okay and I did the right thing. If I had got in here earlier, I could have made presents for Mommer and the young'uns, like Papa done. You take care, Miss Mulcay."

For a moment Kate stared at the phone. Then it hit her like the clouds parting. "That's it!" Kate nearly blurted out. She dialed Phil Brown's number and spoke as soon as he picked up. "Phil, I don't know how to repay you for all this, but there's one more thing I'm going to need to do."

"What's going on, Kate?"

"I found Iris Moon's real killer."

The maid opened the Barnetts' door with a glimmer of recognition.

"Hello, Darlene. May I see Hettie if she's at home?"

Kate was shown to the sunroom, and Hettie appeared. "Sit down, Hettie. There's something I want to ask you." Kate waited until the girl was seated on the love seat. "I know how much you love Beau," Kate began. Hettie looked at Kate but didn't respond. "I also know that Miss Moon had"—Kate stumbled for a word—"*relations* with Beau. I'm sure that made you angry."

Hettie's eyes filled with tears. Suddenly she sobbed, "I didn't kill her, Miss Mulcay! I never meant to. I went over there right after I saw those homeless friends of yours leave, and Miss Moon and I were arguing about how she treated Beau so bad. I may have shoved her, but I never meant for her to get hurt like that! She just tumbled on her high heels right down the stairs and cracked her head. Please don't let them put me in jail!"

Kate felt a surge of compassion. Young love and a quick temper were suffered by more girls than Kate could remember, yet this one had experienced two deaths in just the span of a week. "I'm sure you didn't mean to do Miss Moon serious harm, Hettie, but we'll need to settle this all the same." The girl nodded and sniffled, and Kate thought she saw a look of relief in her eyes.

The cabin seemed cold and lonesome when Kate drove into the yard. She would even have welcomed the gregarious Gandy sisters if they had shown up. But they were probably at the new mall at Alpharetta, which they dearly loved. She should have given them some money so they could shop for their mama and papa. She only hoped their normally spendthrift parents had saved a bit out of the last land sale to give the girls something for Christmas. When she first knew the Gandys, they had parcels of land all around the area, but it had gone, a field at a time, and the money was spent on cars and their double-wide trailer, and Kate wasn't sure there was any left. Once, she had suggested that they put away money for the girls' education, but she found their attention wandering, although they were polite about it. Education didn't loom big on their list of essentials.

She stood at the back door, looking at the lights showing through the woods across the road. In summer she couldn't see the subdivision houses, but when the leaves fell, lights glimmered through the branches along Shine Creek. Nowadays they ran to the red and green, floodlights outlining rooftops and assaulting pines and cedars, while strings of little white lights illuminated shrubs and small trees.

Kate looked at her one gesture toward Christmas decoration—the fat green wreath with its big, often-pressed red velvet bow on the cabin door. It was austere, niggardly. She felt ashamed. She had not even got a Christmas present for Jonathon.

And what about Saint Margaret's spring garden tour? Would it be on, with Jonathon gone? Or would a new rector abandon the project? In her present state of weary discouragement, she rather hoped she would not have to get her sparse patch ready for company.

A cold wind stirred around in the panicles of dried bloom lingering on the ash tree at the edge of the yard, and the Burford holly next to the cabin rustled icily. Pepper came down the path through the subdivision and across the road to greet her. He had been visiting Miss Willie, she knew. He spent no time with the subdivision dwellers, most of whose dogs were of superior breeds. The ancestral background of Pepper was unknown at the Humane Society, whence Kate had sprung him. He loved Miss Willie and felt welcome at her fireside. The old woman now could be seen following him down the path toward Kate's cabin.

"Howdee," she said, her voice muffled by the knitted fascinator she wore, which covered all her face except her eyes. Once, Kate had teased her about wearing a ski mask.

"'Tain't," Miss Willie retorted. "Hit's a fascinator, like womenfolks used to knit and wear agin frostbite."

"Well, then, you could wear it on the ski slopes," Kate had pointed out in fun.

"'Twill serve, I reckon, at any fool place you feel obleeged to go."

Now, walking toward Kate with her pie basket held carefully before her, Miss Willie reminded Kate, "We bound to some Christmas to-do in town, ain't we?"

"That's right. Tomorrow night." Kate wondered if she should warn Miss Willie that they would be going to an abandoned, almost vacant house to be the guests of a couple of grubby sidewalk beggars who had been murder suspects. Of all the people she knew, Miss Willie Wilcox would be the most flexible and accepting. The descendant of rebellious Scots who settled in the mountains and ignored laws against non-tax-paid whiskey and seasons for fishing and hunting, she was not shocked by law violators. Perhaps murder would shock her, but she would be the judge of innocence or guilt, trusting her own judgment of character above that of courts and juries.

"How did you know I was home?" Kate asked as Miss Willie drew up even with her in the yard.

"I didn't know," the old woman said. "Pepper knowed. I saw him lift his head and wag his tail, and I knowed he heard you come home."

"Well, let's go in the house," Kate said, taking the old woman's basket. "I'll turn up the furnace and pour us a glass of sherry."

The old split-oak basket was heavy, and she

maneuvered it carefully past the kitchen door, not tipping it. Whatever Miss Willie brought deserved to be handled tenderly.

"'Tain't nothing but some sweet pertater pies," Miss Willie said deprecatingly. "I made two and tucked in some jars of my blackberry jelly. Men ain't no hand at making sweet things. I brung them tonight because tomorrer I'll have to tote a jelly cake and some hog head cheese."

"Oh, Miss Willie, you shouldn't have gone to so much trouble," Kate protested. "Shag and Warty will feast on these things. I'll drop them off on my way to work tomorrow, and we can take the other stuff you have when we go. A friend of mine is going to take us. You'll like him—Philip Brown, a lawyer. I've known him a long time, and he offered to escort us to the party."

Miss Willie tilted her head and examined Kate's face with one of her rare, knowing smiles. Kate was aware of what she was thinking. A replacement for the preacher man, of whose departure Miss Willie with her antennae must have already heard.

"It's not what you're thinking," she said firmly. "Phil Brown and I have worked together on a lot of things, but there's nothing . . . personal between us."

Miss Willie dropped the subject. "I'll be a-going," she said. "See you tomorrer."

At the last minute, Kate called Philip Brown and offered to meet him downtown. Driving out to the country to get them and then bring them home was a hard, traffic-beset drive, she decided, and besides, Phil with his oblivious turn of mind would probably get lost. He seemed relieved, agreeing to meet the women in front of the newspaper building.

"Lordamercy, the people!" the old woman exclaimed as Phil drove them down Whitehall Street. "Where did they come from? Where are they going?"

Kate and Phil laughed. Whitehall, once a major business street, boasting Atlanta's leading department stores as well as the *Searchlight* building, was hanging on with cheap chain shops and a heavily black trade. It was busier tonight than usual, with families, package-laden and stroller-pushing, with teenagers shrilling and galloping through the slower crowd, with the ring of Salvation Army bells and the recorded carols pouring out of shabby stores when the doors opened to last-minute shoppers.

By contrast, the neighborhood south of the capitol appeared deserted, and even the streetlights were out on Bass Street. Miss Millicent's house seemed as dark and forsaken as its neighbors, but as Phil pulled up in the alley, Kate saw a faint flicker of candlelight. Then she heard music! Somebody was playing a piano.

Shag met them at the back door, and once they were in the kitchen, they were surrounded. Half a dozen people poured into the room from the dark

dining room and the parlors beyond. They were a ragtag bunch, men and women in frayed and dirty clothes, most of them wearing knitted caps that were unraveling and askew on unkempt, bedraggled heads. One man was on crutches and another, the last to approach them, pushed himself along the floor on a homemade platform resting on skate wheels.

"Lordamercy!" whispered Miss Willie fearfully.

But before Kate could reassure her, she saw that the Bechstein in the kitchen had been cleared and Warty sat before it, his hands outstretched on the keyboard. He struck a note, and suddenly the motley crowd was still, listening to "Jingle Bells." The piano was out of tune, but it was still grand, and Warty could play it.

Shag was trying to make introductions, but the names seemed lost in the cold draft from the big rooms beyond the kitchen. Kate thought she recognized most of the crowd anyhow, street people she had seen selling newspapers, begging, sleeping in doorways.

"They our friends . . . mostly," Shag said expansively. "Evva one of them can make music. We gon' eat and you gon' hear."

Warty left the piano for the stove, and Kate saw at once that she should have brought bowls or dishes of some kind to hold the stew, which was simmering fragrantly. Warty's makeshift dishes were tomato cans, soup cans, tuna fish cans, doubtless retrieved from neighborhood garbage containers but divested of their labels and scrubbed. There was one for every guest, including Kate, Miss Willie, and Phil Brown, who looked squeamish but valiant as Shag pushed a can containing stew into his hands.

"Don't worry," Shag said. "This crowd has et out of cans many a time. In the old days, when we tramped, that was all we had—a can to hold over the fire on a stick." He grinned at Miss Willie. "And sometimes we didn't have no water to wash it."

Miss Willie nodded and tasted the stew with one of the plastic forks Kate had brought days before.

"Rabbit," she said.

"Yeah, ain't it tasty?" responded Warty happily. "Miss Kate found a rabbit for the pot. Don't it add?"

The consensus in the room seemed to be that the rabbit *made* the stew. Kate saw Phil Brown slip his can back on the edge of the stove. She would eat hers if it killed her.

Suddenly from one of the darkened rooms a piano sounded, and the guests nodded and began to sing "The Hungry Hobo." They all seemed to know the words:

I don't feel very hungry. Just bring a couple of
   hams,
A barrel of salt and pepper, and two or three fat
   lambs.
My appetite is failing. Just bring a couple of
   whales,
A hundred pounds of bread, and fifty ginger ales!

There were a lot of verses, and the singers, hoarse and out of tune, were hampered by mouths full of

stew, but they sang on, and occasionally one who
had eaten his fill of stew would take a piece of Miss
Willie's sweet potato pie and slip into a darkened
room. And then another piano would be heard
from.

"Say, Mister Brakeman, how about riding your
choo-choo train?" they sang. There was a song about
rabbit hash and lost loves and one maudlin number
about a hobo who had saved the life of a drowning
child. They sang of outlaws and daring railroad
engineers.

Kate took a moment to pull Phil aside in the
kitchen. "Everything working out okay with Hettie?"
she asked.

"You've kept me busy, Kate, but I think we'll get
her taken care of. Her sentence should be lenient,
because it was clearly an accident."

"And what about Beau?" Kate asked.

"That's a bit more complicated, but he'll probably
still do time for the crime he claims to have committed all those years ago. That is, as long as he contin-
ues to implicate himself in it."

A scruffy man popped into the kitchen with an
empty can, followed by another, and gradually the
emptied cans were put in the sink and the seedy,
smelly men and women began to disappear into the
front of the house. Other pianos started up.
Unmusical though she was, Kate recognized that the
pianos were rickety and run-down. But the tunes
were strong and the singers were diligent.

"I want to see them," Kate whispered to Phil, and
he surprisingly took a small flashlight from his

pocket and steered her and Miss Willie into one of the front rooms. Six of the pianos were in use. In the absence of stools and chairs, the players sat on boxes. The legless man on the roller-skate platform had been hoisted to the only straight chair the house seemed to possess, and when he saw he had an audience, his dirty arm and gnarled hands raced over the keyboard, making boogie music of the old hobo laments.

The others, who had been drawing out mournful bass sounds, lightened up and joined in the lively tempo.

Kate noticed that Phil was smiling and Miss Willie was tapping a foot.

They stood and listened as long as they could bear the cold in the unheated rooms, and then they went back to the kitchen, where Shag was cutting the jelly cake and Warty was thumping away on the Bechstein, in harmony with his pals.

All at once the pianos were silent, and from somewhere in the front of the house, the low, sweet voice of a woman sang:

> There grows a bonnie brier bush in our kailyard
> And white are the blossoms on it.

Miss Willie, listening, whispered the next words: "'Like wee bit white cockades for our loyal Highland lads . . .'"

"You know that song, Miss Willie?" Kate asked in awe.

Miss Willie nodded. "'The Scotch in the Moun-

tains.'" She lifted her voice to new lines: "'He's coming from the north to fancy me,/A feather in his
bonnet, a ribbon at his knee.'"

Kate swallowed hard. The cracked old voice, join-
ing the sweet singer in the front room, was beautiful.
When the song ended, she nodded toward the parlor. "Who is she?"

"Oh, Flippy Nell," said Warty, turning back to the
Bechstein. "She come from the mountains, but she
used to sing—and strip—in a carnival."

"She's lovely," said Kate, and then, to Miss Willie:
"And so are you!"

"She's on dope," said Shag neutrally.

"I don't care," Kate said. "She's a lovely singer. I
want to speak to her."

Later, she wished she hadn't. Flippy Nell was old
and fat and painted up like a roadside strip joint
sign. She had bright-red hair, turning purple at the
part, and her hands, covered with cheap and gaudy
rings, had clawlike nails painted red to match her
hair. Even her fat bosom, half falling out of a
sequined blouse, was very dirty.

"Oh, I liked your song," Kate began. "Would you
sing us another one?"

Flippy Nell smiled, showing an absence of several
front teeth.

"Sure, honey," she said. "How about 'Where art
thou, my love, tonight?'"

"Oh, thank you," said Kate, sad at the appropriate-
ness. She returned to the kitchen.

"Lucky you come back," said Warty. "She totes a
razor and don't like nobody."

Phil Brown heard him and touched Kate on the shoulder. "When this one ends, don't you think we'd better go?"

Kate nodded and listened to Flippy Nell's words: "'My ship is floating on the tide, and prosperous winds are blowing . . .'"

Oh, I wish they were blowing for all of them, Kate thought. She wondered where they would sleep tonight. The shelters had long since filled up and closed their doors. But she wouldn't worry. They apparently were set for the night. When Nell's song ended, Warty struck up "Silent Night," and throughout the dusty, cold old house the dirty, homeless street people touched the abandoned pianos and joined him.

Kate and Miss Willie and Phil eased out the door, saying goodbye only to Shag and Warty. When Phil paused for a stop sign at Georgia Avenue, they could still hear the pianos, now playing "O Come All Ye Faithful." As Warty had dreamed, it was a ghostly sound.

Celestine
Sibley

DATE